BLOKES IN DONEGAL

WINDY MOUNTAIN
BOOK 4

JOHN MARTIN

ABOUT THE AUTHOR

John Martin is an Australian. He used to be a journalist, now he's free to be frivolous.

https://johnmartin-author.blog

CONTENTS

ONE
OPTIC AND OP SHOPS

THE BELL tinkled when the man in the washed-out overalls followed his walking stick in through the door. Behind him was a big man with grey whiskers, who was wearing a red checked shirt and loud tracksuit pants.

Walter 'Goody' Moncrieff looked over the top of his glasses, then stood up. "If it isn't Clarrie Noodle? I was just reading about you!"

The frames displayed in cabinets along the walls looked like they were long overdue for a feather duster. "What can I do for you gents?" Goody walked around to the front of the reception desk. "Don't tell me you're looking for a Tasmanian Tiger *in here*!"

The man wearing the colourful, stretchy pants turned to go. "I told you this was a mistake, Oodles."

Clarrie Noodle reached up and grabbed him by the shoulder. "If you want to actually see that castle of yours, old son ..."

Then he turned to the optician and blew out his cheeks. "Sorry, Goody, you haven't met my business partner." He pointed from man to man and back again. " Goody, Bert Whish-Willson; Wish-Wash, Walter Moncrieff."

Goody smiled and held out his hand. "I recognised you from the photo." He pointed behind him to the newspaper spread open on the counter.

Oodles had first come into this shop on the Slutz Plains High Street in 1972 when he had clumsily broken an arm of his reading glasses in his car door. He lived 15 minutes' drive down the hill in Windy Mountain but this was the only optical business in the district.

Oodles guessed the optician would have been in his early 30s that first time. He had had the look of a fearsome cricket fast-bowler complete with intimidating moustache and an open-neck shirt that showed a forest of dark chest hair and a gold chain around his neck. These days, Goody had taken to wearing a white lab coat to hide the chest foliage that most likely matched the snowy white of the hair on his head.

Let's see? If Oodles was 85 now, Goody had to be in his late 70s. He wasn't just the oldest optician for miles and miles, possibly in the whole of Tasmania, he had become the town's oldest receptionist since his long-time assistant Polly had taken long service leave to do a river cruise on the Danube. He couldn't afford to replace her for three months. So he had a bell installed above the door, which he'd hear on the rare occasion he was out in the back room consulting with a customer. Mostly, he sat at the receptionist's desk and read Wisden.

Oodles took his scratched glasses out of his bib pocket and held them up. "I need replacements, Goody. Wish-Wash needs a new prescription. He's an 83-year-old virgin."

Wish-Wash glared at Oodles. "What are you talking about?"

"You've never had a pair of glasses in your life."

Wish-Wash pointed heatedly towards the window. "How can I be a flaming virgin? Tell Goody about my grandson Rod."

Goody threw a hand to the side of his head with a slap. "I *thought* I had seen someone like you before?"

Wish-Wash broke out in a smile for the first time. "You know my grandson then?"

"No, but I've seen him lots of times crossing the road. He works over at the Travel Agency. You and him, um, share a similar sense of, er, sartorial splendour."

Wish-Wash's smile grew wider. He had just bought those elasticised pants minutes before after he had seen them in the opportunity shop window two doors along. He got as excited as a boy seeing a lolly shop whenever he saw a shop selling second-hand clothes — so he insisted they check out the op shop before going to the optical shop.

Oodles had to watch him model the new trousers. They were predominantly dark green, but with orange swirls.

Wish-Wash was thrilled they felt so comfortable when most of his other trousers felt so tight, but he wanted to know how they looked. What could Oodles say? It was no worse than many of the fashion choices the lard-arse had made.

Wish-Wash had asked the attendant if the shop took trade-ins. He told him the traffic-light-red trousers he had been wearing when he came in had only had one careful owner who normally only wore them to church. Oodles knew this was bunkum. Ignoring the occasional trip to church for a funeral, places of worship were foreign territories for Wish-Wash. Oodles also knew the red slacks were already pre-loved when Wish-Wash had bought them from an op shop in another town. The attendant was having none of it either.

Wish-Wash hid the old slacks in the change-room anyway. That'd teach them, he said. Now they'd have to go to the trouble of throwing them out.

Oodles wondered what made him think his new tracky-dackies went any better with the red flannel shirt he was wearing today and the flip-flops that showed off his gnarly toenails.

Goody switched his gaze from Wish-Wash to Oodles. "How long have you been using that divining rod?"

Oodles looked around the room, wondering where the divining rod was. Only when his eyes settled on the hickory walking stick did he get the joke.

"Oh this? I've only been using it since yesterday. Doc Jenkins wants me to get used to it before we go to Donegal in three weeks' time. We both went for our medical yesterday and Jenko also reckons Wish-Wash needs long-distance glasses. I figure I need new readers. So here we are."

Goody scratched his chin. "Donnygirl? How do you spell that?"

"D.o.n.e.g.a.l. It's in Ireland." Oodles put an arm around Wish-Wash. "My mate here won a couple of air-tickets that were offered as a prize for him doing a DNA genetic est."

Goody leaned in closer and dropped his voice, like he didn't want anyone else to hear and realise he was no longer the fearless fast bowler. "I've given up on flying. The fear of crashing was bad enough, but the final straw was hearing about that bloke who had a fatal heart attack in his seat. No one knew anything was wrong with him until they tried to wake him up when the plane had landed."

"Thanks for that confidence boost, Goody." Oodles shook his head. "That story sure trumps mine. I was only worried about putting my back out again. When Madge was alive, we once flew from Singapore to London sitting up in economy, and my spine hasn't been the same since."

Wish-Wash's chest swelled, though not quite as much as his belly. "You won't have to worry about that. The good news is you can die lying down in business-class capsules these days."

Oodles gave him a dark look. "You're very sure for someone who has never been on a plane."

"Rod brought me some brochures."

Goody frowned at Wish-Wash. "You've never flown? Not even on a prop to Melbourne?"

"Nope," Oodles piped in. "Guess that makes him an extra virgin."

TWO

'TWO YEARS IN THE CLINK, AT LEAST'

"Did you have to say that?" Wish-Wash said when they started walking back towards Oodles's car.

"You can talk!" Oodles was still thinking about what Wish-Wash had told the Mayor two days before. "Anyway, what did I say?"

"You called me a virgin — *twice*!"

"I was trying to lighten the mood. Do you think we would have got such a good deal if Goody had been grumpy? Back in the day we used to call him Good Grief Moncrieff for a reason."

"Why did it have to be at my expense though! I have a reputation to uphold in this town. I could run into my ex-missus at any time."

"You really think she'd recognise you all these years later as the man she had a quickie with behind the dance hall?"

"You make it sound so tawdr—" Wish-Wash stopped abruptly and glared at the park bench on the grassy verge next to the footpath.

Oodles stopped and turned around, then walked towards the bench. The dry grass crunched beneath his feet. The grass had been a lush green when the bench had mysteriously appeared here. But in the past week the sun had beaten down and no rain had fallen, and now the grass was more yellow than green. Oodles stroked the fresh red paint. "You must have noticed this when we arrived?"

Wish-Wash shook his head. "My mind was elsewhere."

"That's one excuse." The car keys jingled in Oodles's other hand. "Those new glasses of yours better be ready in time. You're going to need them in Ireland."

"I've got on fine for years without them."

"Says the man who thought the fourth line of Goody's eye-chart read d i c k h e a d."

"It did." Wish-Wash studied his face. "Didn't it?"

"They were random letters, you drongo. You sure you didn't need glasses back in 1967?"

Wish-Wash stamped a foot. "Why did you even have to bring that up?"

Oodles's attention was drawn to Wish-Wash's feet. He scowled. "When did you last trim those toenails?"

Wish-Wash went quiet and tilted his head. "Hmm, Christmas."

"Only four weeks ago? You're kidding me!"

"No. It was the Christmas before."

"Strewth," Oodles said.

"Are you trying to change the subject?" Wish-Wash pointed to the bench with a shaking finger. "What's this still doing here? It belongs back in Windy Mountain."

Oodles shrugged. "I guess someone has to sift through the evidence first."

"The Mayor's in jail, isn't he? What more evidence do they need?"

James Northan hadn't actually been mayor for some time, but people still called him that as a joke. Members of his family had held a near-stranglehold on the position since his great, great, great grandfather had founded Windy Mountain in 1841, and his daughter Maddie wore the mayoral gown right now.

James was 82, deaf in both ears, and Oodles and Wish-Wash had formed an uneasy alliance with him. He was a cranky old bugger who thought he was better than just about anyone else. But they had been forced to make peace with him because all their other friends had dropped off the perch and the bench really needed a third person on the end.

That was hard enough for Oodles, who had once worked under James's beck-and-call as council works supervisor.

But it was even harder for Wish-Wash, who had never forgiven James for orchestrating his removal from a job he had loved.

In 1967 Wish-Wash claimed to have seen a Tasmanian Tiger in a bus shelter. The reason he was there was quite credible. Wish-Wash then was the town drunk, so he often slept in the bus shelter, but his very occupation also made his alleged siting of an animal believed to be extinct less than credible.

James Northan was outraged. He said the publicity brought shame on Windy Mountain, and took steps to see to it that Wish-Wash was sacked. He claimed Wish-Wash had actually got off easy. His great, great, great grandfather would have hung, drawn and quartered him.

So it was remarkable that years later they agreed to do the DNA genetic test together. Oodles didn't want to know about his family roots. But Wish-Wash was curious because he didn't know quite where he had come from, and the Mayor was cocksure he would get confirmation he was descended from British aristocracy.

When the results were mailed to them separately, it boosted Wish-Wash's self-esteem no end. No matter he was now the co-owner with Oodles of the Tasmanian Tiger Museum and had been on the sobriety wagon for many years, you never really lived down the stigma that you were once the town drunk. But the DNA genetic test gave him new status. It found he was descended from a free-settler from Donegal. More good news followed. He was put in touch with a distant relative in Ireland, who informed him he had inherited a castle in Donegal. A castle! Him?

The DNA results were roughly the same for the Mayor, but the outcome was very different.

He was appalled to find his ancestors also came from Donegal. He didn't believe this nonsense for a second, but it propelled him into making a trip to Hobart to visit the State Archive and Heritage Office. That research made it even worse. He found out his great, great, great grandfather had not only never reached the rank of colonel that he had always been known as in family folklore, he had arrived in the colony with a ball and chain attached to his ankle. At best, he had been released early and might have secured the rank of sergeant. He had been put in charge of a group of convicts exploring the furtherest reaches of the colony so they could raise the flag for England.

The Mayor never shared with anyone his new-found knowledge his ancestor was actually transported as a convict from Ireland.

What he did was go into hiding and join forces with his nephew, a known criminal nicknamed Messerschmitt, to start dismantling Windy Mountain — and the shame — bit by bit.

Signs disappeared, the Colonel Robert Northan Memorial Park bench was relocated to Slutz Plains in the dead of night, the Windy Mountain pub was burned down, wreckers tried to demolish the Tasmanian Tiger Museum, and the big bronze statue in the middle of the main street depicting Colonel Richard Northan astride a big horse was removed under the cloak of darkness.

When the long arm of the law closed in, James Northan turned himself in.

When Oodles and Wish-Wash went to see the Mayor in jail, he blamed the worst crimes on his nephew, who was still on the run.

When they told him they were shortly off to Ireland he had to ask them to repeat it because he wasn't sure his hearing aids were working properly.

When he adjusted them, the aids both gave high-pitch squeals — and Wish-Wash repeated the news with more volume and greater glee.

James's face went even whiter.

Wish-Wash reached over and squeezed his knee. "I wish there was a mirror in here, Jimbo, so you could see the look on your face." He laughed like a donkey. *Hee-haw, hee-haw.* "Tell you what? If you somehow get out of this fix you're in, we're taking you with us." He glanced at Oodles. "Isn't that right, cobber?"

Oodles rolled his eyes. "But we've only got two seats?"

"Two *business-class* seats. I'm sure they'll cash them in for three *economy* seats."

They stopped on the way out and chatted with Sergeant Stretch in the charge-room.

When they got back on to the street, Oodles said, "Why did you have to go and tell James we'd take him with us?"

Wish-Wash laughed again. "Torture!"

Oodles glared at him. "What if he somehow gets released?"

"Come off the grass! You heard Stretch. The Mayor has to be looking at two years' prison at least."

THREE
HE'S CARRYING THE BAGS

THREE WEEKS LATER

"It's very good of you to pick me up first." Oodles watched Wish-Wash's grandson Rod lift the suitcase into the back of the dual-cab ute. He was wearing red trousers and a blue polo shirt with a red hoop around his midriff.

Oodles was wearing his best overalls. He slid into the back seat and rested his walking stick on the inside of his right thigh.

Rod had offered to drive them to the airport in Launceston. From there, they'd fly to Melbourne. Melbourne to Dubai. Dubai to London. London to Dublin, where they would pick up a rental car and drive up to Donegal.

As Rod backed out of the drive, he turned his head. "You know granddad has agreed to come and live with me in Slutz Plains?"

"No way." Oodles opened the window because he felt the air had just been sucked out of him. "Last I heard, he was moving back into the pub now Rog's decided to rebuild it."

"I think he was waiting for the right time to tell you about his new plan. I think he wants to get right away from James Northan after this trip."

"Strewth, how far away does he want to be? Risdon Jail is a long way from Windy Mountain. It's just a crying shame the police haven't been able to catch that nephew of his. No one would mess with James if Messerschmitt was his cellmate."

"Didn't granddad tell you? James Northan has been released. The council didn't want to press charges."

"You're kidding me?" Oodles watched the houses whizz by as they drove down the hill. "He stole the signs, for goodness sake; he gave away *our* bench; he stole the statue. Don't they count for anything?"

"Mayor Maddie Northan reckons he had council permission to do all those things."

"What about the attempt on the museum? And the burning-down of the pub? No one could have approved those things!"

"He says neither of those crimes were anything to do with him. It's his word against Messerschmitt's — and he's obviously not here."

———

As the car approached the museum, Oodles saw two men standing with suitcases on the footpath outside the museum.

As they pulled up, he saw the whiskery one had squeezed into an emerald green suit that was too short in the legs and showed off his red socks, and a red body shirt. The clean-shaven bloke was almost a head shorter and was wearing one of the designer grey pinstripe suits he always wore. White shirt, blue tie. *Groan.*

Behind them was Moose, who was leaning on his crutches. Next to him was Joffa, who could pass as Moose's younger brother until he began talking and his accent gave him away as being from somewhere else. Joffa had his arm around Katy, who was tall for a woman, but looked diminutive beside him. Rounding off the farewell party was the Texan teenager they had nicknamed Awesome Sauce.

Oodles and Rod undid their seatbelts and got out.

Oodles took Wish-Wash aside and whispered in his ear. "He's really coming with us?"

Wish-Wash smiled. "He's agreed to come along as our carer."

Oodles shook his head, then turned and extended his hand to Moose. "It's all yours now," he said, nodding towards the museum. "I only hope you and Joffa and Katy can turn it around after all that's happened."

"You sure about this?" Moose said. "It's very generous of you. You didn't deserve what happened." He looked to Joffa, then to Awesome Sauce.

"Don't blame them, old son. Life's too short to burn with regret. Move on. That's what we're doing. I can wait to burn some rubber on those Irish roads."

Moose lowered his voice. "I can't believe you've decided to take the Mayor with you!"

"Nothing to do with me. I've just found out myself," Oodles said.

"Do me a favour," Moose said. "Lose him in a crowd in a busy airport. Better still, push him out of the plane over an ocean."

"You don't mean that, old son!"

"Oh, I do. Windy Mountain would be a much better place without him."

They were interrupted by Wish-Wash's booming voice addressing the Mayor. "I hope you've turned your hearing aids on?"

They turned to see Rod unclipping the tarp and his hand moving towards the handle of the first suitcase.

But Wish-Wash reached out and stopped him. "That's Jimbo's job."

FOUR

'HAVEN'T I SEEN THOSE TROUSERS BEFORE?'

NOTHING WAS SAID for the first mile of the journey but Oodles could tell by the way Wish-Wash kept looking sideways something was on his mind.

Oodles had a good view from where he sat in the back alongside the Mayor.

Finally, Wish-Wash couldn't contain himself. "Where did you get those, Rod?"

Rod took one hand off the steering wheel as the gum trees flew by on either side of the road. It sounded like he was patting one of his trouser legs. "Like them, granddad?"

Wish-Wash growled. "I've told you before not to call me granddad. It makes me sound old."

"You *are* old, Bert," came the Mayor's voice from the back seat.

Wish-Wash turned around and glared. "I'm only a year older than you, Jimbo! But I'm in much better nick. Didn't I tell you? I don't want to hear a peep out of you until you're beckoned!" Then he noticed the silver laptop computer the Mayor was holding and his voice grew weaker as he ran out of breath. "Why did you have to bring that? We're going on holiday!"

The Mayor looked down. "This? Some of us like to stay in touch with the latest news."

Wish-Washed sucked in oxygen. "Christ Almighty, can't you do that on your smartphone? That, and all your email?"

"Oh, for goodness sake, Bert! Only common people email on their phones." He tapped the computer. "Anyway, there is much more to my computer than just its email capability."

"You're not one of those old blokes addicted to internet porn, are you? Because if you are, we're going to need different room arrangements."

The Mayor raised his voice indignantly. "Really, Bert! What are you implying?"

"Nothing. I'm just trying to work out why you'd want to cart that computer around the world. Don't they have newspapers in Ireland?"

The Mayor sighed. "Some information I need you can't find in your common provincial rag." He stroked his laptop lovingly. "This device gives me up-to-the minute information about my share portfolio."

"I thought you were skint!"

"I am. It's a struggle just to pay my accountant."

"Typical! You mean to tell us—"

Wish-Wash didn't finish what he was saying. What was the point? He turned back to the front and returned to the subject of Rod's traffic-light red trousers. "I used to have a pair just like them. Where'd you get them?"

"The op shop in Slutz Plains sold them to me."

"Christ Almighty, no wonder they're familiar." Wish-Wash pounded his own chest with his right hand. "I *knew* I had seen them before. They're the ones I left there!" .

"Oh gross!" came the Mayor's voice from the back. "I do hope you washed them, Roderick."

Wish-Wash's angry glare over his shoulder was enough to make the Mayor reach up and turn off both of his hearing aids.

Wish-Wash shook his head, turned around and addressed Rod again. "When did you buy them?"

Rod kept his eyes on the road. "Nearly three weeks ago. I had been watching a nice pair of tracksuit pants displayed in the window for weeks. Wednesday afternoon is when they do price reductions, so I popped across the road to check if they had been marked down further. I couldn't believe someone else had bought them. I think they could see I was angry when I went inside, which is why they offered me these ones for five dollars."

"Five dollars!" Wish-Wash unwrapped a nicotine tablet and started chewing on it. "You've been had. Surely you remember seeing me wearing them! I would have sold you them for four dollars, and I would have washed them first."

"How do you know they didn't wash them?" Rod tightened his grip on the steering wheel.

Wish-Wash sighed loudly. "What time did you get to the shop?"

"About 4.30pm — after the travel agent closed for the day."

"That's all the proof you need then. They wouldn't have had time to wash them when I had only left them in the change room half an hour before. I'm surprised they even had time to find them because I thought they were pretty well tucked away in that rubbish bin. Which reminds me, who even peels an orange in a change room?"

Oodles laughed. "Is that why the green track pants you got have orange swirls, old son?"

"Very funny," Wish-Wash said. "You wait and see. When I wear them in Ireland a lot of people will be jealous."

"Strewth, you're not telling me you've packed those!"

Wish-Wash lifted his right arm and held out the jacket sleeve between his thumb and forefinger. "I'm only wearing my best threads on the plane."

"Where did you even get that green suit and red shirt anyway?" Oodles said. "It makes you look like a giant parrot."

"Where do you think I got it?"

———

It all made sense now. Wish-Wash had made the trip to Slutz Plains with Oodles just a few days ago. The reason for the trip was to pick up their new glasses. But the lure of the op shop was too great for Wish-Wash and they had gone their separate ways. When Oodles came out of the optician's shop with the two pairs of glasses each in a spring-loaded red case, Wish-Wash was standing on the footpath holding a large plastic bag.

When Oodles had asked what was in the bag, Wish-Wash trotted out one of his favourite sayings: it was for him to know and for Oodles to find out.

Guess he had just found out.

"You don't think that green suit used to belong to Father O'Boring, do you?" Oodles said, as the car rolled on. "That would explain why the sleeves aren't long enough and the trousers are at half-mast."

Wish-Wash shook his fist. He had never had time for the short-arse Father John O'Rourke, who had died when the Catholic church was torched.

Oodles could see he had opened a wound, which was all the more reason to keep Wish-Wash on the back foot before he could hit back. "Why aren't you wearing your new glasses?"

"Why aren't you?"

"Mine are reading glasses, yours are for long-distance. Goody wanted you to start wearing them full time straight away."

"Yeah, well, it won't do me any harm to wait until I get to a part of the world where no one knows what I look like anyway."

Oodles started making chicken noises. *Beerk, beerk, baaaaarh.*

"Who are you calling chicken?" Wish-Wash said.

"I didn't call you anything," Oodles said.

"No, but you were implying it. If you ask me, you should be more worried about yourself anyway."

"Nothing wrong with my eyesight." Oodles turned to the Mayor. "Doc Jenkins said I should be able to see an ant's balls from 10 yards away."

The Mayor frowned. "What did you say?" He fumbled with the hearing aids. "THERE IS NOTHING WRONG WITH MY EYESIGHT."

"Why are you shouting at me?" Oodles said. "I never said there was."

Wish-Wash craned his head over to the back seat again. "I was talking more generally about your health, Oodles. Pack all your meds, did you? You have the potential to ruin this trip. Not many people live past 85."

Oodles swallowed. "Jenko gave me a clean bill of health. Do you think he would have done that if he thought I wasn't up to this trip?"

"Maybe he is happy to get rid of you? It couldn't be good P.R. for his business if some of his patients die on him in Windy Mountain."

The Mayor feigned indignity. "That's a terrible thing to say, Bert!"

"The truth hurts, Jimbo," Wish-Wash said. "But at least Jenko had the good grace not to be there to see Oodles off — which is more than I can say for Moose's diplomacy. I reckon the only reason he was there was to make sure you left town."

FIVE
'GO ON, BIG-NOTE, SHOW US WHAT YOU'RE MADE OF'

As THEY PULLED into the car park at Launceston Airport, Oodles felt nostalgic and sad.

He and Madge had flown out of Launceston on Boxing Day 1975 bound for Western Australia. The itinerary had them catching a Russian ocean liner from there and spending five or six days at sea on the way to Singapore, from where they'd fly on to London.

But the Russian ship wasn't waiting for them in Fremantle, which caused them some anxiety. A replacement, the M.S. *Kota Singapura*, did arrive — three days and many missed heart-beats later. But good came out of the delay and change of ship. They spent New Year's Eve celebrating at sea, which was an experience they had never anticipated.

He'd never forget a crew-member dressed as Neptune hamming it up with a plastic trident at the crossing-the-equator ceremony. Somebody had pushed Oodles into the pool, which had been a welcome respite from the heat and a funny talking point for years right up to Madge's death in 2015.

The old men wheeled their suitcases into the terminal. The Mayor also carried his laptop, as Rod trailed behind juggling their carry-on bags. The Mayor's carry-on bag was nearly as big as his suitcase and, judging from the way Rod was struggling, perhaps heavier.

"What have you got in there, Jimbo?" Wish-Wash asked.

"I couldn't fit everything into my case," the Mayor said.

"Like what?"

"That's on a need-to-know basis."

"You don't think I need to know? Who's paying for your ticket?"

"I thought you said you got them for free?"

"I did. But two *business-class* tickets! You ought not underestimate the big sacrifice Oodles and I made in trading them in for three *economy* air-fares?"

"I never asked you to. You volunteered."

Wish-Wash flicked flakes of dandruff off the shoulder of his lime green suit, then stared coldly at the Mayor. "Yeah, well, the less said about that, the better. Just remember, Jimbo, Rod won't be with us to carry the excess bags for the rest of the trip — that'll be your job."

The Mayor stared back. "I thought you meant you wanted me to carry all our passports."

"What?" Wish-Wash frowned.

"I am the best qualified for that job. I'm the most seasoned traveller among us so I know exactly when to produce the relevant documents."

"What about Oodles? He's travelled, too."

"Once! For six weeks. I hardly think having a little statue of a Grenadier guard standing at attention on his mantlepiece qualifies him to be a travel guide."

Wish-Wash rolled his eyes. "I've waited 83 years for my first passport. It'd be just like you to lose it on purpose to ensure they'd leave me on the tarmac watching my own plane take off."

"Wouldn't happen," the Mayor said. "No passport, no entry on to the tarmac. You'd be watching through the terminal window."

"Whatever, wherever. You're not getting my passport." Wish-Wash parted his coat slightly and spoke from the corner of his mouth. "Anyway, it's safe as houses where it is." He patted his chest. "It's hidden away in my money pouch, close to my body."

"You're wearing a money pouch?" The Mayor tutted. "No one wears money belts any more. If the security men see you patting your chest like that, they're going to suspect you have explosives strapped to your body."

Oodles butted in. "Don't listen to him, old son. You won't need to show your passport for this first leg anyway. You can duck into the dunny in Melbourne and take it out there."

"Haven't you heard of CC-TV cameras!" the Mayor said.

"In the blinking toilet cubicles?" Oodles screwed up his face.

"I wouldn't put it past them. It probably takes your photo whenever you hit the flush button. Next thing your photo is on the Big Brother computer and the CIA knows how many sheets of toilet paper you used."

"That would be a gross invasion of people's privacy," Oodles said.

"They're very strict on security these days."

By now, they were at the ticket counter and Wish-Wash herded the Mayor to the front. "Go on, Big-Note, show us what you're made of then."

The Mayor turned his back to Oodles and Wish-Wash so he could talk to the woman behind the counter.

He turned around. "The girly here says she needs to see everyone's ID."

Oodles reached into his jacket pocket and took out his wallet. "My driver's licence do?" He extracted it and handed it over to the Mayor.

Wish-Wash went pale. "You know I haven't got a driver's licence!"

"Your passport will do," the Mayor said.

Wish-Wash hissed. "I'm not taking my passport out here! Christ Almighty, why do they even need to see my ID anyway? I know who I am! Isn't my word good enough for them?"

"Please yourself," the Mayor said. "Just don't blame me when you're left behind in the terminal." He lowered his voice. "You wouldn't be in this position if you had given your passport to me."

Wish-Wash turned to Oodles. "You said I wouldn't even have to show my passport yet."

Oodles shrugged. "No one ever asked for it in 1975."

Wish-Wash undid the first two buttons of his shirt and pulled out the money pouch hanging on a cord around his neck, unzipped it and pulled out his shiny new passport. He slammed it into the Mayor's hand. "I want it back, OK?"

"You need to relax," the Mayor said. "If the security people see you sweating they are going to want to know why. "

He showed the ID documents to the woman behind the counter and she began inspecting them and hitting a flurry of keys on her computer.

The Mayor lifted his suitcase on to the conveyor belt and watched the weight indicator. It was over the limit slightly but the woman in the uniform said that was OK because they were connecting with an international flight. She tagged it and it disappeared into the tunnel.

"Next," she said.

Wish-Wash pointed to his suitcase. "You're on again, Jimbo."

The Mayor looked around, hoping to summon Rod, who had plonked down the carry-on bags just behind them. But he had wandered off and Oodles could see he was now looking at a paper in a newspaper stand across the terminal.

The Mayor sighed and lifted Wish-Wash's suitcase into place. The display window showed it was lighter than his. She tagged it and pressed a button to send it on its way.

Oodles didn't wait for help. Wish-Wash was carrying on like a pork chop. Oodles didn't care for the Mayor either but he would only become more intolerable if pushed too far.

Oodles's suitcase was lighter again.

Inside were two more sets of overalls, three Y-fronts, three shirts, three pairs of socks, two jumpers, one warm duffle coat and one pair of running shoes. Not that he did any running these days but they were light and comfortable. Goodness knows what the others had packed. The Mayor had about 12 identical grey suits, all tailor made from merino wool. He couldn't have packed them all. Could he? Oodles was pretty sure what kind of things Wish-Wash had packed. It wouldn't end with the green and swirly orange trackie-dackies. Ireland was about to be inflicted with a wardrobe full of fashion crimes: novelty flip-flops, blue singlets, floral shirts and jumpers no self-respecting sheep would admit donating wool to.

He watched the attendant tie a tag on to his case and send it on its way.

She handed back the ID documents and boarding passes to the Mayor, and pointed the way to security.

"Any take-on bags?" she asked as the Mayor redistributed the passport, driver's licence and boarding passes.

The Mayor held up his laptop, then pointed to the floor.

Luckily, she couldn't see the size of the bags on the ground. Oodles's bag was big enough, but he wasn't about to entrust six weeks' worth of medication to a suitcase that might get left on the tarmac in Dubai and somehow get rerouted to Mumbai. He also had an e-reader in there. People were always surprised an 85-year-old would even have that but Oodles found it practical. It meant he could carry dozens of books with him and crank up the type size if he couldn't find his reading glasses. He had packed those in his carry-on bag, too, along with a fresh shirt, a change of jocks and socks, and his toiletries.

Wish-Wash's bag was bigger again. Oodles knew he liked to read sci-fi books so no doubt there were a few paperbacks in there, including the latest guidebook on Ireland.

But the Mayor's bag was something else again.

What could he possibly have in there?

They found out at security when the old men emptied their pockets and sent their bags and belongings through the X-ray machine.

SIX

HAVEN'T I SEEN THAT HEAD BEFORE, TOO?

"Is this your bag, sir?" asked the large stone-faced officer on the other side of the conveyor belt.

James Northan had come through the screening frame without a beep and had jostled for front position as the carry-on bag came through. With one hand on the handle, he could hardly say it wasn't his. He just nodded.

"Would you mind opening it?" The security man looked like a Pacific Islander, who probably played prop for his rugby team. Worse, he looked like a man whose team had just lost a big game.

"Is there something wrong, officer?"

"I just need to take a look."

"Didn't the X-ray machine already do that?"

"It showed up a large mass. I just need to see what that particular object is."

"In front of all these people?" The Mayor had sweat beading on the back of his neck.

The officer nodded towards a side office. "Would you prefer we do it in private? Just stay where you are while I wait for another officer to be available to stand in as witness." He took the bag away from the Mayor and lifted it on to a table behind him.

The Mayor looked around at his companions, who had both passed though the X-ray frame and had already picked up their luggage, tipped their coins back into their pockets and replaced their belts.

"I'm sure it's just routine, old son." Oodles had felt sure he'd be the one who would hold them up at security. He knew people who were sick of always setting off the X-ray machine with their knee replacements. Oodles still had both his kneecaps but he also had a titanium rod in his leg that surgeons had implanted a couple of years before when he had broken his fibula and tibia on an ill-fated fishing trip. So he was pleased when he passed through the screen without a beep.

Wish-Wash just smiled at the Mayor and made a movement like he was putting on imaginary rubber gloves.

The Mayor turned back to the sullen officer. "Second thoughts," the Mayor said quickly. "I have nothing to hide. Feel free to inspect it here. I expect you're skilled at looking into bags without having to pull everything out."

"Please yourself." The officer carried the bag to another table along the line, where they both could stand, and the Mayor moved up. Oodles and Wish-Wash followed close behind. Rod hadn't been able to come into the security area but he was standing like a red beacon just beyond the barriers. He could see something was going on and looked puzzled.

"Unzip the bag, please, sir, " the man in the uniform said. "Place the contents on the table."

The Mayor gulped. "All of them?"

The officer nodded.

First came a neatly folded spare white shirt.

Then came a blue tie, which looked identical to the one he was already wearing.

Next came a ball of grey socks.

Then a pair of white Y-fronts appeared, which contrasted with his red face.

The Mayor pulled out a toiletries bag, which the officer picked up off the table and unzipped. He took out a large tube of toothpaste and examined it carefully as he rotated it, before popping the lid and smelling the contents. "You do know this exceeds the allowable size?"

"It's toothpaste! Is that what the X-ray machine flagged?"

The officer shook his head. "No, but I'm going to have to confiscate it, sir. Keep going."

"For heaven's sake, I've only got one more thing left to unpack. If you look into the bag, you can see it. Haven't you embarrassed me enough?"

"Sorry, sir, you still have the option to do it behind closed doors."

At this, Wish-Wash resumed the putting-on of his imaginary rubber gloves — this time with disgusting sound effects he made with his mouth.

"Oh, whatever."

Other passengers were lurking, just waiting to see what came out of the bag next.

It probably came as a shock to them. It certainly did to Oodles.

Out came a large bronze head, which the Mayor slammed down on the table with a clang.

Oodles had seen that head before.

It had been on top of the statue that had gone missing from the middle of the Windy Mountain High Street.

In that rendition, Colonel Richard Northan was an Errol Flynn-lookalike astride a big, rearing horse. In the forlorn version on the table, his head didn't even have a body attached, let alone a steed.

The Mayor turned to Oodles and Wish-Wash to offer an explanation. "I only wanted to take him back to his traditional home."

"Strewth," Oodles said. "I thought the statue was going to be melted down."

"Still is." The Mayor jutted out his jaw. "The proceeds will go into the council's consolidated revenue. But no one's going to miss a head!"

"You sure about that?" Wish-Wash said. "That's theft in my book."

"You don't think I have some ownership of my own relative's head?"

"But it's not his actual head, is it?" Wish-Wash said. "You don't even know what he looked like. Christ Almighty, we now know he wasn't even an officer. He was an ex-convict in charge of other convicts."

The Mayor turned even whiter. "Did you have to remind me? Don't you think that stain has tarnished our family reputation enough!"

"Hmm … hmm." This clearing of the throat came from the other side of the table.

The Mayor turned round to see the officer's mean mouth had formed into a smirk. "You can't take this on the plane, sir."

"Why not? It won't be hurting anyone."

"That's debatable." The officer pointed at the larger-than-life head. "This could be used as a weapon. It could do some damage if it was bludgeoned against someone's head." He paused. "But there are other issues. The bag probably wouldn't fit into an overhead locker and there is the issue, as your friend points out, that this head might be stolen property and you're trying to spirit it out of the country."

The Mayor stiffened. "Are you going to arrest me? I have to tell you I have friends in high places and they'd probably be happy to re-deploy you to a remote airstrip somewhere in the outback. Thought about where you'd like to go, have you?"

The officer's smirk turned into a scowl. "I have no jurisdiction to arrest you, sir, but I do have the authority to prohibit you from taking this bronze head on to the plane. You have three options." He counted on his fingers. "Option one: we confiscate the object. Option two: you leave the object in the care of someone who's not flying with you. Option three: you choose not to fly either."

The Mayor turned to his friends.

"I like option three," Wish-Wash said. *Hee-haw, hee-haw.*

James Northan spat out his words. "You're the last person I'd ask for advice, Bert. If you'd just listen for a change, all I wanted to ask is if your grandson was still here."

Oodles pointed. "He's waiting to wave goodbye to us over there."

Wish-Wash squinted that way. "Is he? I can't see him."

"Strewth, he looks like he's on the way to fight a fire in those trousers. This is another good reason you should be wearing your new glasses!"

"I can't. They're packed in my suitcase."

The Mayor looked to the other side then back to the officer. "How can I get this to Rod?"

The officer pointed to a door. "I can let you out that way but you'll have to come through security again."

The Mayor picked up the bag, handed his laptop to Oodles to mind, and off they went.

The next time the two other old men saw him, he was walking back through the security frame.

He cleared it without a beep and stopped near the end of the line to collect his jacket, his belt, his keys and his change.

Oodles handed him back his laptop. "Is your bag still coming through, James?"

"No, I left it with Rod. I had no choice. He said he wasn't going to carry a head through the airport for everyone to see."

"Won't you need a change of clothes?"

He exhaled deeply. "No, I'll be fine."

SEVEN

'LOOK WHAT YOU'VE DONE, YOU STUPID OAF'

WISH-WASH WAS JUST STARTING to get himself comfortable when Oodles leaned across the Mayor in the middle seat "All right, old son?"

He was mindful this was his first flight.

The big man popped another nicotine tablet into his mouth. "It's a bit bumpy."

The Mayor winced. "Will you stop squeezing the back of my hand, Bert!" he said. "Can't you wait until we at least leave the ground."

The turbo prop was taxiing to the end of the runway. Oodles had the window seat and Wish-Wash was next to the aisle, so they had no choice but to speak over the Mayor.

The plane came to a halt on the end of the runway. The main noises in the cabin were music and gushing air.

Wish-Wash let go of the outside armrest he had been squeezing and wiped his sweaty brow with his hand. "Christ Almighty, I could do with a smoke."

"I thought you were giving up?" Oodles said.

"How did you give your pipe up so easily?"

"Doc Jenkins said it was the only way I was going to get rid of my cough."

"But you stopped like …" Wish-Wash clicked his fingers. "… that?"

"The doc gave me a choice. Cold turkey or dead duck."

Wish-Wash reached up and turned the air vent on high then fixed his eyes on a flight attendant standing in the aisle and unfurling the tube of a yellow oxygen mask.

At the end of the safety demonstration, he put up his hand.

"Where are the parachutes, love?"

She smiled, walked up the aisle and placed a hand over his right hand. "Relax, sir. As soon as we get airborne, I'll bring you a nice cuppa."

"And a parachute?"

She shook her head. "Will you settle for a muffin?"

"I normally have a couple of chocolate digestive biscuits with my tea," he said, hopefully.

"You'll have to pay extra for those," she said.

They were interrupted by a P.A. message from the captain. Would all cabin staff take their seats.

The flight attendant headed to the front of the plane as the roar of the engine got louder.

Ashen-faced Wish-Wash squeezed the back of the Mayor's hand even harder and looked sideways to his companions as the engine roared. "Are we about to crash?"

"Hardly," the Mayor said. "We still haven't taken off! Oh, this is ridiculous!" He used his free hand to switch off both his hearing aids.

This didn't deter Wish-Wash. He turned to Oodles and shouted above the engine. "Why would I have to pay for a couple of bickies?"

"User pays these days, old son," Oodles shouted back. "It's a wonder they don't make you pay for the life-jacket under your seat."

"That's another thing I don't understand. Why do they provide life-jackets and not parachutes?"

"In case we ditch into Bass Strait."

"Is that likely?"

"Not at all. But best not to think about it. If we do survive the crash into icy water, I doubt the life-jacket is warm enough to stave off hypothermia for long."

The plane was leaving the ground. The roar became a whine as it lifted up and up.

Oodles turned his head and peered out the window.

The rental-car and public parking lots of Western Junction looked like they were full of matchbox cars, the roofs took on a doll's house look.

The plane tracked over Evandale, on to Launceston and up the Tamar River towards open water and Melbourne less than an hour away.

When the plane levelled, the engine noise abated somewhat and the seat-belt light pinged off, the tea and coffee trolley started inching down the aisle.

By the time it reached the old men, the plane had left the land-mass of Tasmania and was well over Bass Strait.

The Mayor reached up and turned on his hearing aids in expectation.

All three men lowered their trays and ordered tea. They got muffins whether they wanted them or not.

Wish-Wash was just raising his cup to his mouth when the plane hit an air pocket.

It's hard to know who screamed loudest — Wish-Wash as his life flashed before his eyes, or the Mayor who was scalded with hot tea over his white shirt, blue tie and the lap of his trousers.

———

"Look what you've done, you stupid oaf." The Mayor began dabbing himself with his paper serviette and the one Oodles offered him.

"You think I did it deliberately, for Gawd's sake. I got a little dribble on my shirt, too." Wish-Wash dabbed at himself with his own serviette.

"Where?" The Mayor looked over. "I can hardly see it. You spilled the bulk on me on purpose. You knew I'm the only one who hasn't got a change of clothes."

"And who's fault is that?"

"It was your grandson who insisted on me leaving the bag with him. What was I supposed to do? Carry my spare clothes on to the plane under my arms?"

"You shouldn't have tried to smuggle out the bronze head in the first place."

The Mayor waved a finger at him. "It's really none of your business what I do with my property."

"But it wasn't your property, was it? The taxpayers of Windy Mountain paid for that statue."

"But it depicted my great, great, great grandfather. Don't you think that entitles me to some ownership?"

"What were you hoping to achieve by smuggling his head to Ireland?"

"If you must know, I was planning to give him a decent burial in Donegal. Yes, history has embarrassed my family by pumping him up to be more than he actually was. But it's time to let bygones be bygones."

Wish-Wash made a noise with his lips like a deflating balloon. "Come off the grass. The only reason you'd want to bury that head would be so you could piss on the grave."

"Don't be so crass, Bert!"

"Maybe if you pissed on it enough, it'd grow the first set of balls there has ever been in your family."

The Mayor opened his mouth to speak but the only noise that came out was a strangled gargle.

"You're just lucky I'm feeling generous," Wish-Wash said. "I knew there was a reason for me to pack two spare sets of clothes in my carry-on baggage."

EIGHT

'DON'T BLAME ME IF YOU START SMELLING LIKE A TEABAG.'

THE MAYOR TOLD Wish-Wash he could stick his spare clothes.

The big man stuck out his bottom lip. "Please yourself. But don't blame me if you start smelling like a teabag."

The Mayor continued dabbing at his soiled shirt. "If you just let me out, I'll go to the bathroom and clean myself up as best as I can."

Wish-Wash glared at him. "You must be joking! I'm not going to risk you unbalancing this plane by walking around."

The Mayor suffered in silence for the rest of the flight. He turned off his hearing aids again.

But Oodles couldn't help thinking he must have been mightily uncomfortable with all those tea slops getting colder against his skin. Even if his white shirt dried, the tea stains would make him look like a walking Rorschach Test when it came time to shuffle out of the plane and into the bright lights of the terminal, and he knew the old ponce would just hate that.

Wish-Wash didn't look that comfortable either. He winced every time the plane hit turbulence and he clenched his eyes shut as they began descending. He clapped when the plane touched down and he made the sign of the cross when the engines were turned off at the gate in Melbourne. He must have seen that done on a movie because he certainly hadn't learned it in the church he never went to.

He had recovered his equilibrium, though, by the time they joined the throng walking purposely along the concourse. They stopped in front of a monitor to check on their next flight.

James Northan was pleased for the breather. He had actually been happy to carry the two carry-on bags because he positioned them to hide his stained shirt from public glare. But he complained all the way down the concourse how damn heavy they were, and he looked relieved when he was able to dump the bags on the floor.

The screen told them they had more than eight hours to wait until their plane left for Dubai.

James Northan looked down at the large brown stain on his shirt. "Do you think they'd let me access my suitcase?"

"I doubt it, old son," Oodles said. "The luggage is checked right through to Dublin."

The Mayor tugged at his soiled shirt. "Surely they'll bend the rules when I tell them who I am!"

———

They watched as the Mayor pleaded his case to the woman behind the airline desk.

Oodles and Wish-Wash were sitting on two plastic seats 15 yards away. Airports are full of hubbub and regular P.A. announcements. *Cedric Smith please report to Gate 3. Your aircraft is ready to depart.* So it was too noisy to hear what was being said but they saw the Mayor wave his passport. The woman took it from him and opened it — but next thing she was shaking her head.

The Mayor was shaking his head, too, when he walked back to them with his laptop tucked under his left arm. "She said it's not possible, you believe that?" He put his computer down on the ground next to the other bags and fixed his gaze on Wish-Wash. "This is all your fault."

"I said I was sorry, didn't I?" Wish-Wash nodded at his bag on the floor. "The offer still stands — you're welcome to borrow some of my spares."

The Mayor looked up at the roof. "Lord, do I have any choice?"

"Of course you do," Wish-Wash said. "But if you decide to stay grotty, don't expect us to talk to you on the next plane. We'll pretend not to know you." He turned to Oodles. "How long did you say the flight was, cobber? Fourteen hours?"

Wish-Wash bent down and unzipped his bag, and pulled out a faded Hawaiian shirt.

He threw it to the Mayor.

James Northan unravelled it and screwed up his face. "Not this one. Dear Lord. Didn't you say you had two shirts?"

"I did. Two of everything. My carry-on bag is like Noah's Ark. But you're not getting the green shirt. That's colour co-ordinated to go with my suit."

The Mayor looked down at the shirt. "Look at it? It's five sizes too big!"

"It's clean, washed and paid for," Wish-Wash said.

"You can say that again. You've washed it so many times in the past 25 years, the pattern has nearly faded away. Remind me again what colours it used to be."

Wish-Wash snatched the shirt back and held it up to the light. "Purple with yellow pineapples, see. If you look closely, you can still make them out."

"People will laugh if they see me wearing that. They'll think I've come dressed as a pizza."

Wish-Wash chucked the shirt back at him. "They'll laugh more if you stay with the Earl Grey look."

The Mayor sighed. "I can't even wear a tie with this shirt."

Wish-Wash puffed out his chest again. "Going open-necked will do you more good than harm. How do you think I get all the chicks?"

Oodles tried not to laugh. He knew the only chicks Wish-Wash ever got came from Roses supermarket, wrapped in tin-foil with two extra drumsticks.

Wish-Wash produced something else from the bag, which you don't see in airport terminals every day.

"You'll be needing these, too." He was holding outstretched a large pair of silk boxer shorts. They were blue and adorned with pictures of yellow ducks, which stopped passers-by in their tracks.

The Mayor waved his hands frantically. "Put them away. Now," he gasped. "If you think I'm wearing your second-hand underpants, you have another thing coming."

Wish-Wash looked wounded. "What are you talking about? I bought these especially for the trip. I've never even worn them." He threw them at the Mayor.

James Northan rolled his eyes as he removed his passport from the pocket of his shirt, which looked like it now bore a map of an undiscovered country.

He thrust the passport into Wish-Wash's hand. "Here, mind this."

Then he stormed off towards the gents to get changed in the privacy of a cubicle.

———

"This must be a misprint." Wish-Wash was looking inside the Mayor's passport.

He lowered it so Oodles could see. It did indeed seem strange. It said the holder was Doctor James Northan.

This was the moment the Mayor emerged from the gents and their eyes were drawn by the Wish-Wash mini-me coming their way. The difference was the faded purple and yellow shirt had never been matched up to grey suit trousers before.

His glare told them he wasn't happy with what he saw across the corridor. "Who gave you permission to look through my passport?" he shouted.

"You never said I couldn't," Wish-Wash said when the Mayor came closer. "But now that I have, explain this. Since when did you become a doctor?"

"That? If you hadn't been so blotto in 1990, you would have read about it."

Wish-Wash glanced at Oodles and frowned. "Do you remember him doing a medical degree? I thought he was the Mayor in 1990."

"Not that kind of doctor, you ignoramus," James Northan said. "The University of Tasmania bestowed upon me an honorary doctorate. A PhD."

"So you're not a real doctor like Doc Jenkins?"

"I never said I was." He tried to snatch the passport back but Wish-Wash raised his hand high above the Mayor's head.

"Oh, this is very childish. Give me that back now."

"What are you going to do to me? Use your stethoscope as a sling shot?"

"Why would a doctor of philosophy even have a stethoscope?"

Wish-Wash continued to hold the passport high. "Don't you think it's misleading to call yourself a doctor in your passport?"

"You'd do it too if you knew the potential advantages."

Wish-Wash squinted towards Oodles. "What's he talking about?"

"Oh really!" the Mayor said. "You can't be that naive? You've never heard of an upgrade?"

Wish-Wash looked hard at him, still holding the passport high.

"Put it this way. If an empty seat shows up in business-class, who are they more likely to offer it to: a big green and red galah or a distinguished doctor?"

"Who are you calling a galah?"

"Who do you think?"

"No wonder your wife left you."

"What?" The mayor's face dropped even more. "I got over that years ago. Why would you even bring that up?"

"Why do you think? Prue's no longer around to call you an ungrateful mongrel, so someone's got to do it."

The Mayor rolled his eyes. "She might have called me a lot of things, but never that."

Wish-Wish lowered his outstretched hand. "Anyway, how will the airline know you're a phoney doctor. You're plain old mister on the plane ticket." He slapped the passport into the Mayor's chest. "All three tickets were issued to me, remember?"

The Mayor pointed to the airline desk. "I thought you would have seen me show my passport to that girlie."

"You tried to deliberately trick them?" Wish-Wash searched the Mayor's eyes.

James Northan smiled. "I knew there was fat chance they would give me access to my suitcase. The real goal was to make sure they saw I was a doctor." He rubbed his hands together. "If it works, I'll have heaps of room to lie down in business-class. Better food, better wine lists, better entertainment system, bags of giveaway goodies. I'd say it's worth a shot, wouldn't you?"

"You didn't explain to them you weren't actually a medical doctor?"

"Why should I? They didn't ask."

NINE
GETTING DOWN TO BUSINESS

When they reached their row, the Mayor's face collapsed when he realised he was expected to be the man in the middle again. "You think I want to sit next to the clumsiest person on the plane again!" he told Oodles with wide eyes.

Wish-Wash, who had just lifted his bag into the overhead locker, was affronted when he heard this. "I don't know why you didn't just stay in jail, Jimbo, and make the world a happier place."

"Very funny! It's going to be a long flight. Is it really too much to ask I can get to the other end without being drenched in drink." The Mayor looked down at his shirt. "Not that it would do this garment much harm, it might even improve it."

"That's it." Wish-Wash started sliding over towards the window seat. When he had sat down, Oodles pointed. "In you go, James. Quickly. People are wanting to get past."

"Why can't I at least have the aisle seat this time?"

"Because you can't," Wish-Wash said. "You knew the rules. We cover your fare and in return you take the middle seat and carry the bags, which ought to be a whole lot easier now because you no longer have a carry-on bag."

"I can't remember agreeing to any such thing. Are you just going to add to my so-called obligations the whole trip?"

The seating was a bit more spacious than their first flight. But it was still a tight squeeze for them.

"Lift your bum." Wish-Wash fumbled for his seatbelt. "You must be sitting on my strap."

The Mayor jumped and turned even redder. "Do you mind? If you'll wait just a second I'll find it for you. I don't appreciate being violated."

"Me violate you? That's a laugh! The only interest I have in your arse is you're wearing my boxers." Wish-Wash prodded the Mayor's chest. "And don't forget I WANT THEM BACK."

"Really?" The Mayor wrinkled his nose. "You'd wear underpants someone else has already worn?"

"You are."

The Mayor's eyes popped. His voice rose. "I took you at your word. You said you had never worn them!"

"I haven't. But someone has. I bought them from the op shop at Slutz Plains. I just hope they did a better job of washing them than they did with the trousers Rod bought."

———

The Mayor's first reaction was to switch off his hearing aids but he didn't count on Wish-Wash slapping his hand down each time he tried.

"You're doing that deliberately."

"Too right I am. From where I'm sitting, it's pretty important you hear every word of the safety demonstration."

"Relax, I've heard it a hundred times before."

"But this is different. I want you to be sure you know what you're doing if you have to get me out of here. Do you know how to do a fireman's lift?"

"If you think I'm going to do my back in trying to rescue you, you're dreaming. If this plane goes down it's everyone for h—"

He didn't finish the sentence. The three of them turned their heads to the aisle where a pretty blonde flight attendant stood smiling.

"Which of you is Doctor Northan?" she asked.

The Mayor raised his hand.

"Oh, you?" She frowned as she took in his unusual attire. "I'm pleased to be able offer you a free upgrade to one of the business-class seats, Doctor. Would you care to relocate? I'll help you with your briefcase, if you like."

Wish-Wash raised his voice, "Why would he have a briefcase, love? He's not even a proper doctor."

"Don't you listen to him." The Mayor glared at the big man next to him."He just can't stand the thought I get to get away from the *riff-raff*."

"Who are you calling riff-raff?" Wish-Wash said. "Oodles and I aren't the ones wearing pre-loved underpants and daggy shirts!"

The Mayor sighed and gave Oodles's shoulder a push. "C'mon, let me up." He turned back to Wish-Wash. "You two ought to be glad. It means you'll get a bit more space to stretch out on this *very long* flight."

TEN
HE'S BACK!

No sooner had the flight attendant ushered the Mayor towards the front of the plane, another flight attendant arrived with another passenger in tow.

"We're just trying to distribute the weight better throughout the plane, gents." She zeroed in on Oodles with her green eyes. "You don't mind moving to the middle seat, sir?"

He did actually. But when the young fellow behind her scowled over her shoulder, Oodles made the snap judgement that this bloke wasn't to be messed with. He had to be close to six foot six, as big as Moose and Joffa — but less of a ball of muscle, more of a wall of blubber and with a glare that could wilt flowers.

Oodles moved across and the colossus squeezed in next to him, and placed his bag on the floor under the seat in front.

He put on some headphones and closed his eyes.

Oodles got the impression he'd prefer to be somewhere else as the plane took off and levelled out.

Oodles had known for years he snored, and he knew Wish-Wash could also snort out a pretty good nocturnal symphony — but he had a hunch this bloke would drown them both out.

He only hoped he'd be easy to wake.

Oodles knew his Woolworths bladder would demand a visit to the dunny sooner or later.

The first hour passed OK.

But come the second hour, the escalating gurgles suggested to Oodles the big man was slipping into a deep sleep.

Just as Oodles began mulling over the best way to wake the sleeping giant, the cavalry arrived. The first flight attendant, the blonde with her hair tied up. Behind her was the Mayor. She looked mighty angry, but the Mayor looked absolutely livid. His face was so red it could have passed for the rear end of a monkey.

The flight attendant shook the man's shoulder gently. "Wake up, Mr Highsmith, we need to do some more seat re-distribution." He opened his eyes and looked around like he was struggling to remember where he was.

She smiled across at Wish-Wash. "Would you like to follow me, sir?"

Wish-Wash clung to his armrests. "You must be joking, love? I don't want to be responsible for making this plane crash!"

The Mayor shouted above the drone of the engine. "I told you he is happy where he is."

She turned around. "As if I'm going to believe *anything* you say?" Then she tapped Highsmith's shoulder again. "Can I get you to stand up please, sir? These other gentlemen need to get out."

She locked eyes with Wish-Wash again. "I assure you it's perfectly safe to move around the cabin, sir. This plane is very stable, and it's a very short walk to business-class where we now have a vacancy."

She turned around and gave the Mayor a searing look before turning her head again. "I'm sure you'll be more comfortable up there, Mr Whish-Willson."

"I think you'll find he's quite comfortable where he is," the Mayor said behind her.

She turned on him again and pointed a finger. "Any more from you, I'll relocate you opposite the lavatories down the back. Or, better still, out on a wing."

He screeched. "What have I done?"

"You still don't get it, do you? I think you need to think about it."

When everyone stood up, Oodles seized the opportunity to go to the lavatory. When he returned, Highsmith was occupying the seat by the window, the Mayor was sitting on the aisle and Wish-Wash was nowhere to be seen.

Oodles motioned for the Mayor to move over.

"Do I have to?"

"Rules are rules, old son. Over."

Oodles sat down on the aisle seat, buckled his belt and turned towards the Mayor. "What happened that you're back here, old son?"

"What happened? I'll tell you what happened! This plane now has one more passenger on it than when it took off, and they're trying to blame me."

"Eh? I don't understand."

"Everything was going swimmingly — hot towels, complementary champagne, some polite girly who took my jacket away to hang up instead of me having to scrunch it up in an overhead locker. But then a medical emergency popped up in one of the first-class suites."

"So that's when you told them that you weren't that kind of doctor?"

"Hmm. Not at first." The Mayor's voice rose. "What would you have done if you were given a chance to see in there? First-class has always been above even my means."

He continued his defence. "It would have been fine if the patient had a cold or a bit of motion sickness. But try prescribing two aspirin to a woman about to give birth and see what her reaction is!"

"You did that!" Oodles laughed.

"I wasn't the one who swore like a sailor. They really ought to have checked my credentials."

"What happened?"

The Mayor shrugged. "They told me to return to my seat, that they'd deal with me when the baby was born. I thought that would give me all the breathing space I needed. I mean, my daughter came after a 22-hour labour. This is typical of this generation." He clicked his fingers. "Everything has to happen NOW!"

Oodles snorted. "So they turfed you out!"

"They said if I dared to show my face at that end of the plane again, my life wouldn't be worth living. It's simply not good enough, is it? In the good old days, one could take one's grievance up with the captain, but these days he's locked in the flightdeck so we're at the mercy of these psycho girlies."

He exhaled through his nose. "I'm not done yet though, mark my words. As soon as we're on the ground, I'm going to send an email to the CEO of this airline. When he hears my side of the story I'm sure he'll come grovelling with the offer of an upgrade for the two of us on our return trip."

"Which two?"

"You and I of course. Bert has fallen on his clodhopper feet. That's why he's sitting in the business-class seat that was rightfully mine."

"Fair go! He didn't ask to replace you up there."

"Maybe not, but I didn't hear him decline it either. The waste is he wouldn't even know what to do with a hot towel!"

"You under-estimate him. He'd work it out."

"You think?" The Mayor threw a hand to the side of his forehead like a headache bolt had surged through his brain.

"You feeling all right, old son?"

"I've just remembered I've left my laptop in a pocket up in business-class."

"I wouldn't worry about it. Wish-Wash would know it's yours."

ELEVEN
MESSAGE IN A BOTTLE

"What do you think you are doing?" James Northan gasped.

Highsmith had chugged the final bit of water out of his bottle, now he had unzipped his fly.

"What do you think I am doing?" Highsmith said. "How's a big bloke like me supposed to squeeze into those tiny lavatories?"

The Mayor had panic in his voice. "Can't you hold on?"

"For another 11 hours? If you don't like it, look away."

Oodles had seen TV vision of airforce planes being refuelled in the air and this operation probably required the same kind of precision.

Not that he saw any of what happened next.

The first thing the Mayor did was turn Oodles's way, with his back forming a protective wall.

He was pulling a face like he had just chewed into a lemon.

Even with his eyes clenched shut, he was able to reach up and switch off both his hearing aids.

He was lucky. Oodles had no choice but to listen to the steady stream hitting plastic, changing in pitch as the bottle filled up.

Highsmith's sigh of relief at the end signalled it had been a successful mission.

The fact the Mayor did not squeal suggested there had been no splatter.

Oodles shouted into the Mayor's left ear. "IT'S OVER."

James Northan opened his eyes slowly and reached up and turned his hearing aides back on but continued to remain twisted sideways. "I wish I had stayed at home. This is becoming the holiday from hell."

"You did start the ball rolling, old son. Or should I say you started the head rolling!"

"I told you why I did that, Clarence. I merely wanted to return great, great, great grandfather to his birthplace. That had nothing to do with all the other things that have gone wrong. A person of my pedigree shouldn't be relegated to cattle-class."

"If I was you I wouldn't be talking up your pedigree — not now we know Richard Northan came to Australia on a convict ship."

The Mayor squeezed his eyes closed again. "You're as bad as Bert dredging that through the mud yet again! Isn't having to sit next to this neanderthal torture enough?"

"You're going to have to turn around and look at him at some stage. You can't sit like that for the whole flight. You'll be so stiff they'll have to cut you out of the plane."

The Mayor's eyes flickered open. "He hasn't even washed his hands. Eeew."

"How do you know that when you have your back to him?" Oodles said. "That duffle bag of his could be chockers with packets of moisturised towels."

The Mayor sighed. "I'm still going to report him. If they have big fines for smoking in the toilets, they must have bigger fines for people not using the toilets when they are supposed to."

"You sure you want to make the beast angry?"

The Mayor banged his fist on the hand-rest. "I paid good money for this seat!"

Oodles cleared his throat. "But you didn't, did you?"

"I wouldn't put it past Bert that he set this whole thing up to make my flight as uncomfortable as possible."

"Come off the grass! Wish-Wash had no way of knowing he was going to take your place in business class and a seat would even become vacant."

"You sure about that?" The Mayor folded his arms. "How do I know he didn't mastermind this, right down to the false pregnancy?"

Oodles squinted. "What makes you think it was a false pregnancy?"

"Have you heard a baby crying?"

"Would we even hear crying above all this engine noise? From the front of the plane? You need to sack whoever's writing your conspiracy theories these days."

"You might even be working in cahoots with Bert, Clarence."

"Strewth! What did I just say?"

"He's cleverer than he lets on. Devious! He's probably hacking into my laptop as we speak."

"Wish-Wash? A hacker? Feeling faint, are you? I thought they said masks would drop from the overhead panel if we needed oxygen!"

"You can laugh, but that computer contains lots of confidential details about my business dealings. He might sabotage me in all manner of ways. Delete files. Add bogus files."

"Are we talking about the same bloke? Wish-Wash struggles to work out how to adjust the time on his digital alarm clock. How would he even get past your password?"

The Mayor looked at him like he had a sudden burning sensation in his gullet.

"You do have a password?" Oodles held his gaze.

"Of course I have a password." The Mayor pulled a face as he swallowed. "Do you think I am a fool?"

"Relax then. Even if Wish-Wash finds your laptop tucked away in the pocket, how's he going to open it?"

"Good point." The Mayor unfolded his arms. "But that doesn't explain how I'm going to get that computer back."

"If you're so worried, why don't you just go up there?What's the worse the flight attendants can do to you?"

The Mayor glared at him. "I don't want to take any chances of leaving this plane in bits aboard a spent meal trolley. If a baby really was born on this A-380, that means they can afford to lose a passenger and their manifesto will still read 850 passengers, or however many started the journey."

"You are kidding, aren't you?"

"I haven't lived this long by being reckless. That's why you need to go up there to retrieve the laptop on my behalf. There is a good reason you've already lived three years more than me. You defy the odds with your dumb luck."

TWELVE
FINDERS KEEPERS

OODLES SHUFFLED up the aisle without his walking stick, which was still in the overhead locker. He ducked under the curtain and counted down the rows.

He couldn't see Wish-Wash's head. When he reached the seat, it was obvious why not. Wish-Wash was fully reclining on his back in all his lime green glory. His shoes were off, and his eyes were covered in a Lone Ranger sleep mask. The Mayor's laptop sat open on the side tray.

"Are you awake, Kemosabe?" Oodles whispered.

Wish-Wash raised the mask slowly and looked with eyes struggling to adjust to the light. "Oh, it's you, Tonto. I thought it might be another flight attendant offering me another drink. It's like they know I've given up booze but are trying to tempt me out of retirement."

He pushed a button that raised his seat to a normal sitting position and the hairs in his nostrils disappeared from sight.

"Why are you still wearing your jacket?" Oodles said. "James said they took his away to hang up."

"They did offer." Wish-Wash grabbed his lapel. "But there's no way I'm letting this out of my sight. There's no telling who you can trust these days."

Oodles pointed to the laptop. "James said he left his laptop in one of the pockets."

"He did. But finder's keepers."

"What are you saying?" Oodles frowned. "It's no good to you anyway. It's password protected."

"Yes, it is. But it's no good to *him* now because I changed the flaming password."

Oodles opened his mouth but nothing came out at first. "How?" he spluttered.

Wish-Washed smiled and beat one side of his chest. "You didn't think I knew how, did you? Didn't you notice Katy was giving me lessons?"

"But she wouldn't have taught you how to crack passwords!"

"It wasn't hard." Wish-Wash puffed out his chest. "I got it in three goes, as it turns out. First I tried his birth-date. No dice. Then I tried his daughter's maiden name. I struck out there, too. Tell you the truth I didn't think anyone would be stupid enough to use my third try. But there you go."

"So what was it?"

"P a s s w o r d."

Oodles whistled a rush of air. "P a s s w o r d! Strewth, you know he's not going to be happy."

"What's he going to do? I'm not giving it back, and he hasn't got his security men at his beck and call any more. There are two of us and only one of him."

Oodles chuckled. "Don't get me involved, for Gawdsake. He's already coming up with conspiracy theories."

"OK, but I hope I can rely on you to keep shtum." Wish-Wash touched the trackpad and the laptop came to life. The log-in screen showed a picture of a Tasmanian Tiger.

Oodles gasped. "Where did you get that?"

"I saved it from the internet. Who would have thought you log on this far up in the sky?" He lowered his voice. "The flight attendant had to help me do it, so I guess that means I'm now in the mile-high club."

Oodles cringed. "The Mayor is not going to like looking at that, old son."

"I know. But think of it as a security alarm. Every time we hear him groan, we'll know he's trying to crack the password again."

———

Oodles didn't mind having to turn sideways and suck in his stomach to let oncoming people get past him because it gave him more time to work out what he was going to say when he got back to his seat.

But when the Mayor came into sight, he looked even more pained than when Oodles had left him.

From the look of him, his eyes weren't the only things clenched. He was curled around in a position a yoga expert would admire. Twisted Bandicoot?

Oodles reached across and touched him on the left shoulder of his faded purple and yellow shirt.

"WHAT'S WRONG NOW?"

The Mayor opened his eyes and turned on his hearing aids. "You? He's only doing it again."

"Strewth, I've only been gone 10 minutes. His bladder must be weaker than mine."

"I don't know how long I can sit like this?"

This was the opening Oodles needed. "Good thing I didn't bring back your laptop then. No way can you look at a computer sitting like that. We don't know how many bottles he has in that bag of his."

He sat down and clipped his seatbelt buckle in. "You don't have to worry. Wish-Wash now knows it's in the pocket. He says he'll bring it with him when he gets off in Dubai."

"I'd feel safer if it were here with me."

"I'm not going back up there again, old son. Peopled glared at me when I came through that curtain."

"Told you! Those hostesses are vicious."

"It wasn't them. They never saw me. It was the some of the hoity-toity passengers who looked daggers at me. Anyone would think I was trying to steal some of their food."

"Did you?" The Mayor's eyes were full of hope.

"No." Oodles glared back. "Mind you, Wish-Wash says they have food and drink on tap up there. He says it's like room service."

The Mayor rolled his eyes. "It's completely wasted on a philistine like him."

THIRTEEN
END OF THE LINE

FLIGHT ATTENDANTS BRING the drinks trolley around at mealtimes on planes. On offer is beer, wine, tea, coffee, juice, and water. Who knew Highsmith would order the lot?

Consequently, it was a 15-bottle flight.

The longest the Mayor got to sit back was for about half an hour. It wasn't reclining in the same way Wish-Wash was reclining up front but it was more comfortable than his twist and pout.

Oodles was glad to land in Dubai.

He only imagined how relieved the Mayor was. Oodles had to help him stand up. It's a good thing the other passengers shuffled off the plane because the Mayor was walking like the tin man.

Wish-Wash was waiting for them when they reached the crowded gate.

The man in the crumpled green suit had his bag by his feet and the laptop under one arm. "Christ Almighty, what happened to you, Jimbo? You look like you lost a crooked sixpence in a crooked sty."

"You know what happened? Economy! It won't be happening on our return trip, I can tell you." He pointed to the laptop. "As soon as I can access my account, I'll advise my share broker to sell enough of my shares so I can pay for an upgrade."

"You'd do that for us? Nice."

"I didn't say I'd do it for you. Moron. You're on your own."

Wish-Wash screwed up his face. "You mean bastard. We could have left you rotting in jail."

"All the charges were dropped, remember?"

"That's because your daughter used her influence. I bet some grubby deals were done behind closed doors."

"That's slanderous! Just give me back my laptop."

Wish-Wash took the computer from under his arm and feigned surprise. "This laptop? This is mine."

"Nonsense! You didn't have a laptop when we left Tasmania."

"True." Wish-Wash nodded down towards his bag. "But I didn't have a lot of the things I have now. A toilet bag, full of all kinds of goodies: a tiny tube of toothpaste, a little comb, deodorant, socks … they are very generous in business-class. *Please accept these gifts with our compliments.* The biggest surprise came when I looked in the pocket in the back of the seat." He tapped the computer. "It's not fake either; it really works."

The Mayor looked to Oodles for support. "Tell him Clarence. I left it in the pocket in my haste to get out of there, didn't I?"

Oodles scratched his head. But it was only to give him time to think. It was an easy choice though. Wish-Wash, for all his faults, had always been his friend, James had always been uppity. "Truth is, I don't even remember you bringing a computer with you, James."

The Mayor's mouth fell open. "You liar," he hissed. "That's why you went up front, to tell Bert I had left it up there."

Oodles looked into space. "Nope. That's not ringing a bell. Sure you didn't dream that?"

The Mayor stamped his foot. "Don't be ridiculous, Clarence. You know as well as I do, you've actually got to sleep in order to dream."

"Didn't you sleep, Jimbo?" Wish-Wash smiled. "I had the best sleep

I've had in months. Remind me to lend you my sleep mask. That's another thing they gave me."

The Mayor stamped his foot again. "You can keep your stupid sleep mask. I just want my laptop back."

"I told you: this is mine. I can prove it. Only I know the password."

"Let me see." The Mayor reached out for possession of the laptop.

But Wish-Wash raised it high above his head again. "You can see it when we get to Ireland," he said. "I don't want to waste any more time. They've given me a card that will get me into the business-class lounge where apparently they have free Wi-Fi."

"YOU KNOW THAT'S MY DAMN COMPUTER, " the Mayor shouted.

When Wish-Wash saw people had stopped to see what was going on, he shouted back.

"THE ONLY THING I KNOW IS YOU'RE WEARING *MY* UNDER-PANTS. DUCKY!"

FOURTEEN
WHAT ARE THE CHANCES?

WHEN WISH-WASH LEFT in search of the air-conditioned business-class lounge, taking the laptop with him, James Northan told Oodles he was in need of a toilet.

"Why didn't you go on the plane, old son?" Oodles said.

"I couldn't. I couldn't move a muscle."

Dubai airport was milling with people waiting for planes or fresh off planes, and the early morning sun was beating down on the building with a ferocity even though a clock high above them declared it wasn't yet 7am. Their Boeing 777 to Dublin wasn't scheduled to leave for nine more hours, and the Mayor said there was no way he could hold out that long.

They walked around their part of the terminal. It was vast and busy as billyo. Throngs of people. Could this number of people really be flying? You had to have your wits about you not to bump into someone else. There were smoking rooms, prayer rooms, and lots of gaudy shops selling every type of alcohol known to man, perfume, jewellery, confectionary, electronic gadgets, neck cushions, sunglasses, well, you name it.

Oodles put his bag down and used his walking stick as a pointer. "There's a toilet over there."

"You must be joking," the Mayor said. "There must be three dozen people in the queue. I'm not lining up with all those plebs."

"Please yourself," Oodles said. "But the longer you procrastinate, the longer the line will get. Look. Someone else has just got in front of you."

"Oh, this is the dizzy limit," the Mayor said as he headed off to join the line.

It took him half an hour to get to the head of the queue.

Five minutes later he emerged even whiter than he had been on the plane.

"Something wrong, old son?" Oodles asked.

"I'd rather not talk about it," the Mayor said.

"C'mon, let's find somewhere to sit." Oodles swept his eyes around the near vicinity. It didn't look promising. Perhaps this explained why so many people were queuing up for the toilet. There was only standing room anyway so they might as well be working towards a goal?

"This is hopeless," the Mayor said. "Let's go for another wander. There must be seats somewhere in this airport."

They weren't quick enough anywhere they wandered though. As soon as one gate emptied with a departing flight, faster, younger people swooped on the seats.

"I'm hot, exhausted and I just want to lie down," the Mayor groaned. "I need to shut my eyes for just a minute."

"You're not Robinson Crusoe, old son. But at this rate we'll be lucky to find even two seats together, let alone something long enough for you to stretch out on."

The Mayor put a hand on his back. "I bet Bert is lying on a nice recliner up in the business-class lounge."

"How can you know that?"

"I've flown business-class through Dubai before. It's very nice up there. You can have all the food you want, you help yourself to champagne, and they even have proper toilets."

"What do you mean?"

"You'll find out."

Oodles sighed. "No time like the present." He pointed to another line queued up to another toilet. "I'll just join that line."

He was as surprised as anyone when the people in the queue invited him to go to the very front.

He was back with the Mayor a few minutes later.

"Well?" the Mayor said.

"Well, what?"

"What did you think of the squat toilet?"

"I had a normal toilet. Porcelain and a flush button."

The Mayor gasped. "I was directed to a room that only had a hole in the ground. It had grab handles on the side so you could lower yourself, and a bucket of water with a ladle. It was very humiliating when I came out and saw the people in that line looking at me as if they had been watching me through the wall."

"What can I say? Maybe you just picked the wrong toilet. What did the sign say?"

"It was in Arabic."

"Wasn't that a clue?"

The Mayor looked at him as if he were stupid. "There are Arabic signs all over this airport."

Then his facial expression formed into even more of a scowl. "How come they let you jump the queue?"

Oodles shook his head. "I never asked them. I guess it's one of the perks of being 85."

The Mayor looked up towards the ceiling. "Oh, for goodness sake! Being a senior with an aching back didn't do me any good."

"That's the difference three years make." Oodles scanned a nearby gate. "Look!" He pointed with his walking stick again. "I see two empty seats over there."

They were in luck. Wish-Wash would have insisted the Mayor carry the bags. But Oodles carried his own bag and was glad when the Mayor reached the seats first.

It was good to finally sit down, even if they were only plastic seats.

"How long until the next flight?" the Mayor asked.

Oodles looked at his watch. "Bit over eight hours."

"That long! I don't think I can sit here for eight hours."

Oodles studied the Mayor's face. He had never seen those bags under his eyes before. "What choice do we have?"

"When do we go to the gate?"

Oodles squinted at the nearest board. After a few minutes, he said their flight wasn't even on it yet.

They did both get to stretch their legs in the following hours, but they took it in turns while the other one minded the seats.

It was so hot in the terminal, buying bottles of water was a regular trip.

"You know there's a ski-field with real snow somewhere in Dubai?" the Mayor said when they sat together drenched in perspiration.

"Get away with you," Oodles said. "Snow in the desert? You could cook eggs on the side of this building."

"Amazing what you can do if you have enough money. I've seen the ski field. It's in a shopping mall."

Oodles looked down at his bottle. "This was frosty cold when I bought it, now it's tepid."

A consequence of keeping up their fluids was they both needed more dunny trips.

Oodles had twice as many trips but he accomplished these in half the time of the Mayor.

This is because Oodles on each of four occasions was allowed to jump the queue.

James Northan certainly tried it on. He even borrowed Oodles's walking stick to use as a prop. But poking the person ahead only resulted in angry looks and a flurry of angry words in a language he didn't understand.

Six hours they sat there before Oodles stood up and hoisted his bag on to his shoulder. "Time to get moving." He squinted at the departure screen again. "Terminal 3, gate A."

"Is it far?"

Oodles shrugged.

Turns out it was. They had to catch a train to get there. It was a driverless train which alarmed the Mayor no end. "If they've found a way to do away with train drivers, planes will be next. How will we know there are actually pilots up in the cockpit?"

"For Gawdsake, don't tell Wish-Wash," Oodles said. "He's nervous enough as it is."

But they didn't even see Wish-Wash. Business-class passengers had their own boarding corridor.

He wasn't the one they needed to be looking for, as it turned out.

The Mayor groaned when they reached their row and saw him sitting by the window.

Who knew Mr 15-bottle flight would be going to Ireland, too!

FIFTEEN
ALOHA!

THE PASSPORT OFFICER looked at them oddly when Oodles and the Mayor stepped up to his cubicle in Dublin.

"Dat's a grand shirt but you do know it's 3 degrees outside?"

"Of course I know," the Mayor lied. "I plan to put on my coat."

The officer looked him up and down. "And what coat would dat be, sir?"

This was the moment James Northan realised he had left his coat on the plane.

Oodles saw the distress on his face. "You'll have to go back to the gate and get it, old son?"

"I wish it were that simple." The Mayor looked even more haggard as he closed his eyes. "Trouble is, it wasn't this plane. It was the big plane from Melbourne to Dubai. They took my jacket in business-class and never returned it."

"Why didn't you remember in Dubai?"

"Are you kidding! A coat was the last thing on my mind in that heat." He rubbed his back and sighed. "Good thing I have two identical jackets in my suitcase."

"I hope you've got a raincoat, too?" Oodles said.

It was just after 9pm. The rain had been beating down on the little windows as the plane dropped through the clouds to Dublin Airport.

Lights lit up a dark runway and as the wheels touched down, streaky yellow and red lights from the terminal and other planes and vehicles came into view.

The officer flicked through the first of the passports. "You've come a long way? How long are you planning to stay in Ireland?"

"Three weeks," Oodles said. "We're tourists."

"Are you planning to visit any other countries in the European Union?"

"Possibly France."

The Mayor grabbed Oodles on the shoulder to turn him his way. His face was lit up with a mixture of surprise and excitement. "France? No one has even mentioned France."

"Didn't Wish-Wash tell you we're hoping to do a side trip to visit Disneyland Paris?"

"Disneyland? Don't be ridiculous. Paris is a city of culture. If you two juveniles want to play the clowns and ride the big dipper, that's up to you, but do me a favour and drop me off at The Louvre on the way."

The officer returned their passports and they followed the signs to the baggage collection hall.

On a seat next to the still-empty carousel sat Wish-Wash, who had changed into his green shirt and green socks, in Dubai probably, and now looked like a giant grasshopper with a laptop on his knee.

The Mayor growled, "What are you doing with my computer?"

Wish-Wash looked up. "If you must know I'm sending an email home to the museum to let them know we've landed safely. But I told you. This is *my* laptop. It was complements of the airline."

"Let's see that." The Mayor grabbed at it but Wish-Wash slapped his hand away.

"You want to break it!"

"I can do whatever I want to my own property."

"But you need to respect other people's property. This is the only way we have right now to keep in touch with Moose and the gang."

"That reprobate! He ought to still be in jail, and you're using my computer to communicate with him!"

"Not just him. Katy and Joffa. And Rod. And Awesome Sauce. Do you want me to drop an email to the Windy Mountain Chamber of Commerce when we go to Disneyland Paris. I'm sure they'd like to see a photo of you wearing your Mickey Mouse ears."

"Oh this is beyond the realms of silliness. That's my laptop and you know it, and I've certainly never owned Mickey Mouse ears."

"Really? Your childhood was even more deprived than I thought. You can have a lend of my ears for the photo but no way are you getting your hands on my computer." He turned to the man in the beige overalls. "Is he Oodles?"

What could Oodles say? He shook his head.

They all turned their heads when two familiar suitcases dropped on to the carousel.

The first was Wish-Wash's. The second belonged to Oodles.

SIXTEEN
THE GRAND PRIX TRACK

BECAUSE HIS SUITCASE was lost in transit, the Mayor was forced to wear an old jumper belonging to Wish-Wash.

Oodles guessed the white wool had been tie-dyed with yellow, red and green sometime in the 1960s, and it had lurked in the back corner of an op shop until Wish-Wash had discovered it and christened it Lambsie.

It was nearly midnight when Oodles keyed into the sat-nav the address for Wish-Wash's castle and drove the car out of the rental-car depot.

The Mayor was still complaining as they waited at the traffic lights. "I can't believe your suitcases arrived, and mine didn't," came his voice from the back seat. "I'm beginning to think you arranged all this, Bert."

"Pull the other one." Wish-Wash craned his head towards the back and pointed towards the roof. "I wish I could take the credit for it but I think someone up there is looking after me."

Oodles laughed as he turned on to the motorway. "You think Father O'Boring has put in a good word for you?"

He saw from the corner of his eye Wish-Wash turn his way. "What makes you think that old prick is even up there?"

"He's bound to be. He was a priest, wasn't he?"

"A priest who played around on the side."

"We don't know that for sure, old son."

"You didn't see the photos Gordo and Freddy had? He was doing it with Daisy Rowbottom"

Oodles kept his eyes on the road as he joined the traffic but shook his head. "You haven't heard of Photoshop?"

Wish-Wash pinched his eyebrows. "Do we have to even talk about this? Just thinking about that old Irishman is spoiling my holiday."

"Turn around where possible," a voice said in a rich County Cork accent.

Wish-Wash might have hit his head on the roof if he hadn't strapped himself in. "Where did that voice come from?" He looked around at the Mayor and then back to Oodles. "We've only hired a flaming haunted car!"

"Relax," Oodles said. "It was only the G.P.S. unit giving us directions."

"The what?"

Oodles pointed to the screen on the dashboard. "The Global Positioning System. It tells us which way to go."

"In Father O'Boring's voice?"

"Not his voice. An Irish voice. I guess that's the voice they set it to so it enhances the holiday atmosphere."

"I don't like it. What's wrong with a map? I don't mind navigating."

Oodles turned the car off the motorway. "Like I'd trust you with a map! We might never get out of Dublin."

"And this gizmo is doing a better job, is it? Aren't we already going the wrong way?"

"I must have taken a wrong turn because I didn't hear it properly. It's your fault for yapping."

"My fault?" Wish-Wash raised his voice. "What about Jimbo? He hasn't stopped complaining."

Oodles sighed. "No drama. That's the beauty of G.P.S.s. They're re-route you."

"I should think so. It did root us in the first place."

"What's the hurry anyway? I'm the one driving. What's an extra five minutes going to matter?"

The G.P.S. directed Oodles on to the right road out of town with a quaint lilt.

The Mayor was anything but quaint as he continued his tirade from behind the driver's seat.

Oodles really couldn't blame him.

They had waited for almost an hour at the luggage carousel. By that time, everyone else had collected their luggage and gone. The conveyor belt had long since come to a stop and the luggage hall had emptied.

The delay suited Wish-Wash, who connected to the airport's free Wi-Fi, with the help of the exasperated Mayor, so he could send his email to Katy and co to tell them they had arrived in Dublin safely.

Heaven knows what else he told them.

It took him a long time to write it, and no way did he look comfortable sitting on a green plastic chair hunched over the laptop that really was on his lap. He stared at the keyboard with intensity and picked out the keys slowly with one finger. The last time Oodles had seen him concentrate that hard, he was marking his card in a bingo hall.

When he had sent the email, they went in search of an airline official. Most of them had probably gone home to bed.

They did find one fellow, though he had a bucket and mop. He apologised for the misplaced suitcase though and he told them if they wrote down their address he'd make sure the note reached the right people who'd forward the case once it was found.

This didn't improve the health and temper of the Mayor who complained he was bloody freezing without a coat. This is why Wish-

Wash came to take the tie-dyed jumper out of his suitcase, throw it at the Mayor and tell him to man up.

Next he threw over a ball of lurid pink socks

He unzipped his carry-on bag and rummaged around until he found what he was looking for. He pulled out a red-and-white woollen bobble hat. It was actually a Sydney Swans beanie but the Mayor took one look at said he had to be joking. It would make him look like Where's Wally.

Wish-Wash stuck out his bottom lip. He said the Mayor could bloody-well please himself if he wanted a frozen nut. He locked eyes with Oodles. "We'll be toasty warm, won't we cobber?"

Wish-Wash pulled another beanie from his bag — the brown-and-gold stripes of Hawthorn — and wriggled it on to his head. Oodles donned his red, white and black St Kilda beanie.

They left the address of the castle with the cleaner, and he directed them to the rental car kiosk.

They had to catch a shuttle bus to pick up the rental car from the depot. There, they found another office, and yet another queue. Once it was Oodles's time to be served, there was paperwork to be done.

The rental car came with a G.P.S. — though they called it a sat-nav. It was all paid for by the same company that had paid their airfares as part of the prize package Wish-Wash had won for doing the DNA genetic test. But the rental car manager wanted to see Oodles's Australian licence, and he had to fill in multiple forms.

When that was finally done and he was given the keys, Wish-Wash insisted on packing the car.

Oodles was sure it could have fitted more than one of the suitcases in the boot, but he was hardly likely to take the Mayor's side.

The result was the Mayor had to share the back seat with one of the suitcases and both of the remaining overnight bags — which would provide a constant reminder that neither piece of his luggage had arrived. He had protested, of course, but Wish-Wash had just smiled.

Now they were on the road at last and the Mayor wasn't letting up.

"I'm so tired," he moaned. "I just want to lie down."

"Well, you can't," Wish-Wash said. "If we're not allowed to sleep, you don't get to sleep."

Oodles turned briefly. "I don't mind if you get some shut-eye, old son."

"You must be joking. The ghost of Father O'Boring is just waiting for me to nod off."

"Don't be ridiculous, Bert," the Mayor said. "It's just a robotic voice on the G.P.S.. We can change the settings and get a nice English voice."

Wish-Wash turned to Oodles. "Is that right?"

"Beats me, old son." Actually, he knew fine well it did, but he liked to get the odd one over on Wish-Wash, too. He knew the G.P.S. voice would drive him mad. "I don't think we should touch it and risk buggering it up."

The Mayor must have caught on. He started banging on about the laptop instead. Now that Wish-Wash had sent the email at the airport, James said the joke had gone on for far too long and could he have his computer bag now PLEASE.

Wish-Wash turned around and gave him the rude finger.

Well, said the Mayor, there was no need to be vulgar.

Then he tried another tack. Bert might like him to mind the computer in the back seat so he'd have some extra leg-room.

Wish-Wash banged his fist on the top of the seat. Don't think he didn't know the Mayor was going to try to crack the password? But it wouldn't do him any good because a) he'd never guess it, and b) the laptop was staying right where it was. At Wish-Wash's feet.

"I was only thinking of you," the Mayor said after a while. "Even if you don't want to sleep, you must want to stretch out after so many hours in the air."

"Oh, I stretched out just fine both flights." Wish-Wash turned to Oodles. "What about you, cobber? You OK to drive."

"Yeah, I'm fine — thanks for asking. I got about as much sleep on the plane as I do in my own bed."

"In that case, I think you need a new bed, Clarence," the Mayor said.

Wish-Wash turned around and waved his finger again. "You worry about your own bed, Jimbo. With any luck, my castle will have a dungeon. You better hope it has somewhere to lie down."

"You wouldn't dare put me in the dungeon!" the Mayor hissed.

"If you keep going on like this … Oodles needs a bit of shush so he can hear the Grand Prix Simulator. Don't you Oodles?"

Oodles didn't correct him. Word association! In his head, Wish-Wash was probably fixated on the voice coming out of the G.P.S.. It did sound a lot like the Irishman he called that fat prick. Fat prick? Grand Prix? Oodles could understand the mix-up.

Now they were back heading in the right direction, Wish-Wash asked: "How long will it take us to reach my castle in Donegal anyway?"

"Funny thing," Oodles said. "Joffa told me it's a shade over three-and-a-half hours, but the G.P.S. reckons it's less than two-and-a-half hours."

"And you believe this gizmo over Joffa. He's from Ireland, for Christ Almighty's sake."

"But he's from Dublin. He obviously doesn't know this neck of the woods north very well."

SEVENTEEN
A LONG WAY FROM HOME

Wish-Wash was snoring gently by the time they left the outskirts of Dublin. The Mayor was no better. The noise that came from the backseat was more of a gurgle with the occasional snort.

Neither of them awoke about two-and-a-half hours later as the G.P.S. guided Oodles into a town illuminated by street lights. He changed down through the gears as he slowed down, but the roar of the engine went unnoticed.

What finally roused them was the ghost of Father O'Boring declaring: "You have reached yer destination."

Wish-Wash opened his eyes as Oodles parked by the kerb, faintly illuminated by street lights.

"Why have we stopped?"

"Isn't it obvious? We're here, old son."

Rain was pounding down on the roof. Wish-Wash rubbed his eyes, then wound down the window. But when a blast of wet, cold air came in he wound it up quickly. He turned to Oodles. "You sure we've come to the right place, cobber?"

Oodles used his hand to wipe away condensation from the windscreen, which was starting to fog up now the engine was off. All he could make out were two-ups-and-two downs on either side of the street. "I keyed the blinking address into the G.P.S.. You saw me."

"Did you put in the right address?"

"Of course I did. See." He turned the engine on again and the G.P.S. lit up. It did indeed show the right street address.

But then Oodles realised there was something wrong.

He blinked slowly. "Who knew there'd be two streets with the same name!"

"But we're near, right?"

"Hard to say." Oodles reached over for his glasses case, which were in the console. He put his reading glasses on, and looked at the G.P.S. more closely. "Bugger! We've come to the wrong county. We're in blinking Galway City. I have no idea how far away County Donegal is!"

He hit some more keys. Strewth, it was worse than he thought. He bowed his head, squeezed his eyes shut, and relayed the bad news. It was almost three hours via the fastest route, and a lot longer if they chose to drive along the Wild Atlantic Way.

"My understanding is the castle is on the coast," Wish-Wash said. "Does that help?"

"Yeah, but it's quicker using the motorway," Oodles said.

The Mayor put in his two bob's worth. "I'm all for going the quick way. Sooner we get there, sooner I can lie flat."

Oodles turned around. "You're going to have to drive, James, because I need some shut-eye now."

"I thought you said you slept on the plane," Wish-Wash said.

"I did, but there's a limit. I've been driving for ages. I need a spell."

"Well, I can't drive," the Mayor said. "Even when I used to drive, my Mercedes was automatic. I'd never be able to drive this car."

Oodles looked to his side. "Oh no, not me," Wish-Wash said. "I've never even had a licence. The last thing I drove was a tractor, and that's when I was a little tacker. It has to be 70 years ago."

"If you can drive a tractor, you can drive this," Oodles said.

Wish-Wash shook his head. "I'm done with breaking the law. I had flashbacks just seeing the inside of the jail cell when we visited Jimbo in the clink."

"Really, Bert!" the Mayor said. "You never miss an opportunity, do you? You know that has all been cleared up. It was nothing but a misunderstanding."

Wish-Wash turned his head. "We have a perfect understanding how it was cleared up, don't we Oodles? Family connections. Old school tie. You're nothing but a rotten mongrel."

"Hey, calm down, old son," Oodles said. "We're going to be together on this trip for a long time. It'll do us no good to be at each others' throats all the time."

"You heard him? At least he used to have a driver's licence. He knows his connections would be useless if he was caught driving over here. But he's quite happy for me to risk jail."

Oodles sighed. "No one's talking about jail. If — and it's a big if — the cops pull you over, they'll realise as soon as you talk you're an Aussie tourist."

"Garda," the Mayor said.

Oodles turned his head. "I didn't catch that."

"Garda," the Mayor said again.

"What?"

"That's what the constabulary are called in Ireland. Garda."

Wish-Wash was having none of it. "I don't care what they are called. I'm not going to jail for you blokes."

"You're not listening," Oodles said. "No one's talking about jail. If you do get pulled up, give them some bull about your licence being in the bottom of your suitcase. If they insist on seeing it, make a big deal of unpacking the case. When you fail to find it, say, damn, you must have left it at home. What are they going to do? Transport you back to Van Diemen's Land?"

He rubbed a hole in the condensation on the windscreen again. "Besides, what do you see out there?"

Wish-Wash frowned. "What do you mean?"

"See any people? Coppers? No one's going to know you're having a little turn at the wheel at this time of night. You'll have the road virtually to yourself, too. What could go wrong?"

Wish-Wash shook his head. "It's not going to happen. We will just have to sleep in the car until you've rested up."

"We can't do that," cried the Mayor. "Surely we can find a hotel?"

"Strewth! At this time of the night?" Oodles said.

Wish-Wash looked back. "It's not the end of the world, Jimbo. Sleeping in a car is luxury. You should try sleeping on a park bench!"

"Don't give me that one, Bert. We all know you haven't had to sleep on a park bench for 30 years!" the Mayor said.

"Maybe not. But it's like riding a bike. You never forget."

"But you've forgotten how to drive a tractor?"

"That's different. And the answer is still no." Wish-Wash bent down and picked up the laptop. "Now if you don't mind, I have to write an email."

Oodles rapped the steering wheel. "Who to, old son?"

"Katy and co."

"Strewth, why? You only sent an email to them in Dublin airport."

"They'll be expecting to hear from us again."

"You're not going to tell them I drove to the wrong place?"

"Of course not. They don't need to know everything."

"What are you going to tell them?"

"Dunno. I haven't written it yet."

"No, but you must have an idea what you plan to write."

"Don't you trust me?"

The Mayor interrupted: "This isn't getting us anywhere. But I know this. I'm busting."

Wish-Wash turned around again. "Why didn't you go in Dublin airport?"

"That was hours ago. Besides, I didn't need to go then. I do now though."

Wish-Wash pointed to the fogged-up passenger window. "You heard Oodles. There's no one around. I'm sure you'll find a lamp-post to cock your leg on."

"Don't be vulgar, Bert. You know how I feel about people breaking the law by urinating in public places."

"Please yourself. I've just about run out of clothes to lend you, so if you have a senior-moment accident you're on your own."

Oodles knew the Mayor would have hated hearing that. Wish-Wash was a year older than the Mayor but that was very much splitting hairs when you're both into your eighties, and Wish-Wash never missed a chance to remind the Mayor that he might be in decline. Mind you, the ghost of Father O'Boring must have unsettled Wish-Wash in turn. The priest had popped his clogs at age 92 when Freddy and Gordo torched the Windy Mountain Catholic Church. Wish-Wash was 82 then. He was 83 now but the voice coming out of the G.P.S. was still 92 as far as he was aware, so he knew he was catching up.

"Will you at least lend me that hat?" the Mayor said,

"What hat? The beanie you didn't want earlier? What makes you think you'll be less of a wally here?"

"It's damn cold out there, and you know it," the Mayor said.

Wish-Wash sighed. "Get it out of my bag back there, Lambsie."

The Mayor unzipped the bag and unbuckled his seat belt roughly.

"Good luck with that email, Bert." He slammed the car door behind him.

Wish-Wash and Oodles looked at each other.

"What do you reckon he meant by that?" Wish-Wash said.

"Beats me. Maybe he thinks it'll be flat."

Wish-Wash laughed and opened the laptop, and it glowed brightly. *Hee-haw, hee-haw.* "Good thing I charged it on the plane, eh?"

When James Northan climbed back into the backseat some minutes later, his sodden woollen jumper smelt like it had been reconstituted back to a sheep by the rain.

"I hope you washed your hands," Wish-Wash teased him.

Thee mayor removed the soggy beanie and threw it on to the seat. "You are so funny, Bert!" Then he started laughing. "So how's that email going for you?"

"I've written the first line already, so there," Wish-Wash said. "You know the laptop came with recharging plugs? They think of every-thing, these airlines. They even have USA sockets on the plane for you to use."

"I think you'll find they are called USBs," the Mayor said.

"That's where you are wrong. It's just more evidence this isn't your computer."

"Oh, I give up." The Mayor switched off his hearing aids and returned to his own world. Who knew what went on in his head then?

At least he didn't have to hear Wish-Wash rattling the keys. Though rattle was the wrong word. Wish-Wash knew his way around the keyboard like someone going into a maze for the first time. Tap, pause, tap, a longer pause and a relatively rapid-fire tap-tap every now and then. Oodles had had slow-dripping taps that flowed faster.

About half an hour later, Wish-Wash cried, "Ta-dah".

"Don't tell me you've finished it, old son. Do you want me to give it a squiz."

"Too late, I've already sent it."

Wish-Wash looked down at the screen, and cleared his throat. "Only, it doesn't seem to have gone."

"Why not, do you think?"

"I have no idea."

"Maybe James will know."

Wish-Wash gave a mock shudder and turned around. "TURN YOUR HEARING AIDS ON, YOU DEAF OLD GIT."

The Mayor smiled when he flicked both switches. "Let me guess? The email didn't transmit and now you need my help."

"Something like that," Wish-Wash snarled.

"Seeing as you insist it's not my computer, I'm not sure I'll be any help."

"No, but it is *like* your computer, isn't that enough to go on?"

The Mayor exhaled. "Have you considered you haven't actually got Wi-Fi here."

"It worked fine in Dublin."

"Are you suffering from memory loss?"

Wish-Wash's face reddened. "There is nothing wrong with my memory."

"No? Do you remember seeing the sign in the airport that there was free Wi-Fi there and asking me to walk you through the steps."

"Of course I remember but I thought that password would be good for the whole of Ireland."

The Mayor clicked his tongue. "Bert, Bert, Bert. You'd be better off with a typewriter. Better still, crayons and paper."

"How do I find out the password for this location?"

"I suppose you could walk up and down the street searching for an unsecured network. I doubt the rainwater would do the laptop much good though."

"Quit playing silly buggers, Jimbo," Oodles said. "Where do we need to drive to get Wi-Fi?"

"At this time of the morning?" the Mayor said. "This is your fault, Clarence. If you hadn't gone the wrong way we'd be close to Bert's castle by now. If it's as good as he brags it is, it's bound to have its own Wi-Fi network."

"You don't have to rub it in, Jimbo. Where can we find Wi-Fi around here? Any ideas?"

The Mayor shrugged again. "I don't know. An all-night McDonalds?"

"As in Big Macs? Strewth!" Oodles said.

"Vicki and Velda say they have free Wi-Fi, too."

Oodles looked around at him. "I didn't think you were on speaking terms with your granddaughters."

"I have no choice but to make polite conversation with them at family gatherings."

"You polite?" Wish-Wash said. "I've heard everything now."

"Do you want my help, or not?"

"So how do we find one of these McDonalds in Galway?" Oodles said.

The Mayor shrugged again. "I suppose you could drive around a bit. You might stumble on one."

Oodles yawned. "I might fall asleep at the wheel after a few hours, too. Or run out of petrol. Then we won't be driving around anywhere."

"I know!" This exclamation came from Wish-Wash. "Pass my overnight bag over here, Jimbo. The travel guide I brought with us has all that kind of information. Servos, cafes, pubs. It's bound to list McDonalds, too." He turned to Oodles. "Turn on the internal light."

They were in luck.

One of the outlets was open all night.

Wish-Wash further perused the listing and the life bounced back in his voice. "Wi-Fi, hot grub, hot tea and, looky here, toilets. I was beginning to think I'd have to do a Jimbo and brave the rain."

Oodles turned on the engine and keyed in the address. It was only about 10 minutes away.

EIGHTEEN
LIFE IN THE FAST FOOD LANE

GOODNESS KNOWS what the staff thought when the three octogenarians rushed in through the door — one of them with a rain-sprinkled silver laptop tucked under his arm.

The girl in the peaked hat who greeted them was a lot easier to understand than the cleaner at Dublin airport. But why she said it was a grand night puzzled Oodles. Couldn't she see they had got drenched just dashing in from the car park, and The Mayor's hair was wet?

Wish-Wash placed the laptop on the counter and wiped his face with a white handkerchief. "Do you have Wi-Fi?"

The girl on the other side of the counter nodded.

The Mayor pushed his way to the front. "What's the password?" he said quickly.

But Wish-Wash shoved him aside. "Can you help me with it, love?" He opened the lid and turned the computer sideways so the Mayor couldn't stickybeak. "I'll just log in."

He prodded the keys slowly seven times with his right-hand index finger, then turned the computer towards the girl.

She smiled and said he wouldn't need a password, he'd just need to agree to terms.

"No wucks. Just give me a pen, love. "

"You won't be needing one of those either," she said, reaching over and opening a web page for him. "Just click dat box and press okay."

Wish-Wash nodded his thanks. But his smile morphed into a frown when he studied the menu board behind her. "Hmm, we'll be back to order in a minute."

They adjourned to a far table and Wish-Wash lowered his voice. "We didn't think this through, boys."

The Mayor blew out his cheeks. "I've decided what I want."

"Yes, that may be," Wish-Wash said. "But do you know how you're going to pay for it? Everything on that board is priced in euro's."

"So?"

"So, when have we had a chance to change our money. I've still only got Australian dollars." He looked at Oodles, who nodded. "Yeah, me, too, old cock."

The Mayor's stare intensified. "Haven't you got travel cards or credit cards?"

"You must be joking?" Wish-Wash said. "What bank's going to give me credit."

"Don't look at me," Oodles said. "I don't even trust those cards."

"Incredible!" The Mayor shook his fist. "After everything you've done to me so far on this trip, now you expect me to buy you dinner."

"Technically, it's breakfast," Wish-Wash said. "The alternative is I log in, send the email, use their toilet, then we do a runner. We'd be in the car and making our getaway before they realise."

"Good plan, old son." Oodles shook his head. "There's a big flaw the way I see it though. The rod inside my leg has ended my sprinting days. I don't think we'd be too hard to catch."

Wish-Wash smiled towards the Mayor. "Looks like we'll have to take you up on your kind offer to shout us, Jimbo."

The Mayor blew out his cheeks again. "It wasn't even my idea to come here. Do you think I want to broadcast to my friends that my first meal in Ireland was at a McDonalds."

"Bull dust," Wish-Wash said. "It was so your idea to come here."

"It certainly wasn't. You were the one who wanted to send the email home. I was merely trying to solve your problem. You needed Wi-Fi, I facilitated that. You haven't even said thanks, Bert."

Wish-Wash's smile became broader. "I'll say thanks when I get my Big Mac. And an ice cream sundae with cherries. Oh, and a cup of tea."

"Make it the same for me," Oodles said.

The Mayor glared at him.

"What?" Oodles said. "I *am* driving. I need the energy."

"You two think I came down in the last shower."

Oodles and Wish-Wash exchanged glances. "When was the last shower?" Oodles said. "I don't think it's stopped raining since we arrived in Ireland, which means we're still experiencing the first shower."

He didn't wait for a retort. It seemed like a good time to make first use of the toilets, and he got up and tapped across the tiling floor towards the sign.

When he came back, there were three trays of food and three cups of tea on the table and Wish-Wash was still trying to work out what to do to make the Wi-Fi work. The Mayor was standing behind him looking over his shoulder.

"Oh, for goodness sake, Bert." The Mayor stepped forward and pointed from place to place. "Use the touchpad there to move the cursor there, yes that little box. Hit return, now move the cursor to OK and hit return again. Now, send your email."

Wish-Wash looked up at him. "When you move away, I will."

"For goodness sake, why would I want to see your stupid email?"

"I might have something in it about you."

"About me? Let me see."

Wish-Wash slapped his hands away. "I can write what I like on *my* laptop."

"You know fine well it's not yours. Anyway, haven't you heard of the laws of libel? You certainly can't defame me and hope to get away with it."

"Can't I? This email is addressed to Moose and the gang. If I won't show you it, what are the chances of him ever showing it to you. This means you'll never even know what I wrote."

The Mayor raised his eyes. "Why are you sending anything to that overgrown oaf? That hooligan ought to still be in jail. I doubt he can even read."

The Mayor crossed to the other side of the table and sat down in time to see Oodles unwrap his burger.

He looked down at it without enthusiasm. "These Big Macs look bigger on the adverts on telly."

The Mayor rolled his eyes. "That's because that's not a Big Mac."

Oodles pulled the bun apart and examined the contents with suspicion. "What is it then?"

"It's an egg and bacon McMuffin."

Oodles kept staring. "Really?"

"Yes, really."

"Wendy does a better job of breakfast than this at the Wind Tunnel Cafe," Oodles said.

"That's highly debatable. Anyway, if you look at what else is on the tray you'll notice something Wendy has never, ever had on her menu. A hash brown each."

Oodles screwed up his face. "I thought hash was an illegal drug!"

"Oh, for goodness sake! You must have heard of hash browns?"

Oodles picked his up, pulled back the bag partway back and eyed it suspiciously.

"Vicki and Velda rave about them."

"But what is it?"

"Just try it, and work it out for yourself."

Wish-Wash, his email sent, joined in the conversation. "You don't actually know what's in them, do you?" He seemed to notice for the first time there was no ice cream sundae on his tray and shouted. "You stingy mongrel bastard! You didn't get us anything we actually asked for!"

"That's not true. You both got cups of tea."

"But no Big Macs, no ice cream. We asked you to do one little nice thing for us …"

The Mayor took a bite of his McMuffin and swallowed. "I'm not made of money, you know! I'm a pensioner who has to count his pennies just like you two."

"But you're not a normal pensioner, are you?" Wish-Wash said. "You're a pensioner with a share portfolio and a family dynasty that owns half the properties in Windy Mountain."

"I don't own them; my daughter does. And my accountant will tell you: my interest in shares is nothing more than a hobby — which, I might add, I can no longer indulge in because someone, and I shall mention no names, has commandeered my computer."

Wish-Wash sprayed flakes of bread as he spoke. "Don't expect me to say thanks now."

Wish-Wash turned to Oodles, who was sipping his tea. The large uneaten portion of his McMuffin laid on his plastic tray alongside his untouched hash brown. "How are you feeling now, cobber? You feel up to driving?"

"I feel 100 per cent better, thanks. The bright lights and tea have revived me."

Wish-Wash wiped his mouth. "I'll just go to the little boys room then, and we can hit the road. My castle in Donegal awaits."

NINETEEN
A MAN'S CASTLE IS NOT ALWAYS HIS HOME

THE CASTLE CAME into view when Oodles drove down the side road.

It was nearly 8am but the sun rises late in Donegal in the middle of winter, which is why the tower was dark against the sparking sea.

The silhouette rose high above the lush green countryside. From the top, the views would have been commanding. In the 15th century, no ship could possibly have sneaked up on vigilant lookouts.

"Wow, that's stunning," Oodles said as he drew closer and changed down the gears.

"You have reached yer destination," Father O'Boring's ghost announced. The G.P.S. had directed them through the village about a mile away, and south until the turnoff. Now Oodles was parking beneath the huge eastern wall.

"Is this is?" The Mayor asked, as they all got out.

"Christ Almighty, what were you expecting?" Wish-Wash said. "A troop of Grenadier guards to welcome us."

"No, but I wasn't expecting the building to be merely a keep. You bragged it was a castle."

"You're kidding me, right?" Wish-Wash pointed upwards to the jagged battlements around the top of the limestone tower. "In the olden days you'd be dodging arrows by now."

"That doesn't make it a castle. A castle has to have other buildings, defensive walls, moats … where are the spikes?"

"The what?"

"The spikes! Where you used to display the severed heads of your enemies."

"Don't give me ideas, Jimbo." Wish-Wash glared at him. "You're just jealous I've inherited a castle and you haven't."

"Nonsense. It's just a garden-variety keep. I just hope my room is not at the top. I could do without climbing up all those stairs."

"I reckon you're in luck then. Dungeons are normally in the basement, aren't they Oodles?" Wish-Wash pointed to the top. "Thing is, though, you will have to carry *our* luggage up there first." He looked sideways at Oodles. "How many floors to you reckon there are, cobber?"

"Hard to tell … no, wait … the windows should tell us." Oodles looked progressively upwards and counted under his breath. "I make it five," he finally said.

The Mayor squinted as he looked up. "I can't even see glass in any of those windows."

Wish-Wash swept his hand through his hair. "You just can't help yourself saying negative things, can you? The sun hasn't hit them yet. In half an hour's time you'll probably need to put your flaming sunnies on to cope with the reflections."

"Don't expect me to be your mule taking your bags up there," the Mayor said.

"I think the word you're looking for is *ass*." Wish-Wash waved a finger at him. "Are you now reneging on the one thing you agreed to do if we brought you along on this trip?"

"No one mentioned five sets of stairs."

———

When they went around the side, they saw something in front of the door.

"My suitcase!" the Mayor cried.

"Bugger me," Oodles said. "How did it get here before us?"

The Mayor walked towards it and turned his head. "It obviously didn't take a detour like us, Clarence."

"Lucky you!" Wish-Wash smiled as he said it. "You've got another case to carr—"

The Mayor yelled.

"What's wrong, old son?" Oodles said.

The Mayor threw open the lid. "I've been robbed! Everything is gone."

Oodles rubbed his temple. "Everything?"

"Yes, every-damn-thing. My two spare suits. Shirts, ties, jumpers. Even my socks and underwear. Gone, all gone." He turned the case Oodles's way."See? It's empty." The lock had been smashed and someone had gouged the side of the case.

"Do you reckon the airline delivered it here like that, old son?"

The Mayor stood up and threw his head in his hands. "If they did, I'll make sure someone's head rolls."

"It's your word against theirs anything was ever in that case," Wish-Wash said.

"Nonsense, they weighed it at the start. What did they think I had in there? Heavy air? Come on, let's get inside. I need to ring my lawyer and lodge a claim with my travel insurers. Aside from the stolen clothes, this is a very expensive suitcase. It might even be beyond repair?"

———

Oodles turned to Wish-Wash. "You're still not wearing your glasses, for Gawdsake."

"All in good time. They're packed away in my suitcase."

"I thought you'd want to get a good look of the inside of your castle? Strewth! Got the key?"

Wish-Wash shrugged. "They knew when we were arriving. My guess is they left it open."

When Oodles turned the handle, it flopped in his hand. He pushed the door open and turned around to the other old men. "Someone has broken this lock, too."

"Probably the same scoundrels who stole my belongings," the Mayor said. "Some welcome!"

The smell of urine hit them as soon as they walked through the doorway, and the morning light beat down on them.

The three of them looked up.

Not only were there no floors, and no staircase, there was no roof.

The rain started to pelt down again.

Oodles's glasses served as a shield. But Wish-Wash and James Northan copped thick drops in their eyes.

———

Wish-Wash was the last to get back to the shelter of the car. When he opened the door, it was obvious why. He had stopped to place a handkerchief on his head.

Oodles and the Mayor merely looked like drowned rats. Wish-Wash looked like a drowned rat with a white monogrammed handkerchief on his head. They weren't even his initials in the corner — probably evidence the op shop in Slutz Plains had expanded its range.

He deflected the stares quickly though by sniffing as soon as he sat down. "What's that smell? It smells like wet dog."

The Mayor, who now had an extra, albeit empty and battered Louis Vuitton suitcase to share the back seat with, said: "You think I like wearing this jumper?"

Wish-Wash turned towards the back. "You do know the colours in the tie-dye are running!"

The Mayor looked down. "Oh Lord. That's all I need."

Oodles was using his handkerchief to wipe his glasses, and sighed as he turned his head. "Don't listen to him, James. He's pulling your leg."

"That'd be right." The Mayor brushed a bead of water from Lambsie. "Instead of trying to deceive me, why don't you tell us, Bert, what we're going to do now about accommodation?"

Wish-Wash raised his voice: "You can't blame me for this! All they told me was I had inherited it. No one told me the castle was in disrepair."

"You didn't think to ask them?" the Mayor said.

"Why would I?" Wish-Wash said. "If I had known, I would have taken up free accommodation in the village. It was offered as part of the prize."

Oodles broke into a smile. "All's not lost then, old son. Can you tell them you've changed your mind?"

"I doubt it," Wish-Wash said. "It's too late now I told them we'd rather have three nights in Dublin before our flight home."

"You told them what?" the Mayor hissed.

"Joffa told me whatever we do, we can't miss Dublin."

Oodles and the Mayor glared at him from different directions.

"Fair suck of the sav," Wish-Wash said. "They were good enough to change the two business-class tickets to three economy-class ones, and they paid for the rental car while we're in Ireland. They've already sent me the chits, so I'd say the B&B in Dublin is already locked in."

"Can't you tell them you've changed your mind about Dublin?" the Mayor said. "Surely they'll understand."

Wish-Wash raked his damp hair. "Look, we didn't have to bring you on this trip, you know? If you had bothered to enter the competition and won, we probably wouldn't be having this conversation right now. And why? Because I very much doubt you would have invited Oodles and me along. And remind me what your Donegal ancestor left you? Not a castle, that's for sure. "

Wish-Washed let that sink in then tapped the top of the seat. "Pass my bag over, Jimbo?"

"Why?"

"Why do you think? I'm going to try to find you a dry jumper. But if I come across my travel guide first, tough. I'm hoping it recommends a B&B in that village we came through."

TWENTY
THEY'RE SELLING THE MUSEUM?

OODLES PULLED up outside the B&B in the main street and gave it the once-over.

"Looks quaint," he said.

"It's not a castle," the Mayor sulked.

"Will you let up," Wish-Wash said. "If you really don't want a hot shower and a warm bed, you can just sleep in the car." He opened the door and Oodles got out the other side. The Mayor followed them.

Good thing he did.

The proprietor wanted a photocopy of someone's credit card for surety, and Wish-Wash pulled the Mayor to the front of the counter.

The Mayor looked aghast. "This is just a loan, right?"

"Of course, of course."

"And don't forget you need to reimburse me for breakfast."

"Don't push it, Jimbo," Wish-Wash said. "Oodles didn't even eat all of his."

"But you ate all of yours."

"Doesn't mean I enjoyed it."

Their back-and-forward was interrupted by Shamus clearing his throat. "Have you got yer passports, gents?"

Oodles and the Mayor produced theirs promptly but Wish-Wash had to turn around and retrieve his from the pouch under his clothes.

They were shown to their room upstairs — a clean unpretentious room with three single beds and an en suite.

Shamus told them where the dining room was. Breakfast was between 7am and 8.30am. Would they be wanting full Irish breakfasts?

Had they come far? Oh, dat fecking far? If they wanted lunch, the pub up the street put on good meals. Early evening, there'd be a warm peat fire burning in the guest lounge. And they were welcome to use the guest kitchen downstairs. They had the place all to themselves because visitors weren't abundant this time of year. Where else were they going? Dublin? Oh, grand. He was from Dublin. He had married a Donegal gal.

He walked over to a panel on the wall and switched on the heater. It would take a few minutes to warm up.

He told them the Wi-Fi password.

Anyting else? Oh, if they saw his chiselers around — Donal aged 10, and Mary, nine — he hoped they wouldn't have that fecking dog with dem again. He had told them time and time again, the manky mutt didn't belong to dem and had his own home to go to.

When he had gone, the Mayor sat on a bed and started taking his shoes off.

"What do you think you're doing, Jimbo?" Wish-Wash said.

The Mayor looked up at him. "I'm pooped. You wouldn't begrudge me first shower?"

"Whoever is ready first gets the first go at it. But you need to bring the bags in first."

The Mayor saw red. "It's not enough you made me pay for this place?"

"You can't have it both ways," Wish-Wash said. "It's a loan, remember?"

The Mayor retied his laces. "Fine! Give me the car keys, Oodles?"

He caught them and headed for the door.

As he turned the handle, Wish-Wash spoke up. "Better bring my bags in first." He was sitting on another of the beds, unbuttoning his shirt, and smiled when their eyes met. "As I said, whoever's ready first, gets first go at the shower."

———

The Mayor had only retrieved Oodles's bags when Wish-Wash had finished his long shower.

He had somehow locked the keys in the car. They had asked Shamus to call roadside-assistance but they'd have to wait two hours for help to arrive.

Wish-Wash wasn't as angry as Oodles expected.

"I'll just have to check my emails." He laid down on the bed and opened the laptop. He didn't seem to mind he was stark naked.

"Can't you put on a towel?" the Mayor said.

"You don't have to look." Wish-Wash tapped the side of the computer. "It's not as if anyone else can see."

"Not if you don't accidentally start the webcam, they can't. That computer has a mind of its own."

"How do you know that? You still think it's *your* old computer, don't you? It's not. The airline gave it to *me*."

The Mayor sighed. "If you say so. But I've read that hackers can even start webcams remotely these days, so I'd cover up if I were you."

Wish-Wash laughed. *Hee-haw, hee-haw.* "They're going to get a surprise if they're expecting to see a young sheila with her clobber off."

Oodles, who was getting ready for his shower, joined the laughter and this double chorus of guffaws infuriated the Mayor.

"Don't say I didn't warn you," he said.

Wish-Wash sighed. "How's a man supposed to concentrate. I need to tell them we're here."

The Mayor changed down his tone of voice. "You don't need help with the Wi-Fi password, Bert."

"I've worked it out, thanks. I'm not a moron, you know!"

"Just trying to help."

"You can help by giving me some shoosh, so I can write this email."

"Of course," the Mayor said. "You'd be dying to tell them the castle is actually a ruin."

"Oh, yes. I'm going to tell them that!" Wish-Wash clicked the track-pad. "Can you imagine what Moose would say? He'd die laughing."

"I can only hope," the Mayor said.

"You're going to be disappointed." Wish-Wash kept squinting at the screen. "The two emails in my inbox would indicate he's alive and well."

"I didn't even know Moose knew how to send email," Oodles said. "You're sure they're not from Katy?"

"No, they are definitely from him. They're from a gmail account, not the museum address."

"What's he say, old son?"

"Bear with me. I'll open them."

His lips moved as he read the screen, then he looked up. "You're not going to like this. They've had an offer for the Windy Mountain Tasmanian Tiger museum. Someone called Mr Sin has offered them cash. Moose wants to know what we reckon."

"I'll be buggered," Oodles said. "How come no one wanted to buy it when it was actually for sale? It's not really our decision to make now though. We gifted the museum to them, so it's their good luck."

"Pig's arse," Wish-Wash said. "They can't just sell it. We put a lot of work into that museum and we deserve the lion's share of the proceeds."

"Let it go, is what I say. We got out of there with our health in one piece. We don't need the money."

"Speak for yourself."

Oodles picked his towel up from the bottom of his bed. "What's the other email say?"

Wish-Wash clicked the trackpad again.

"It's worse than we thought." He buried his face in his hands. "Now someone called Wong has put in a rival offer."

The Mayor sniggered. "Trevor Wong, eh?"

Wish-Wash was almost frothing at the mouth as he tipped himself off the bed, thumping his bare feet on the carpeted floor. "How do you even know his first name? Moose didn't even mention it in his email."

"Oh, Maddie's been negotiating with him for months," the Mayor said. "He's a software developer who wants to set up a micro-chip factory, and she's offered some very attractive tax concessions."

"What? Do away with the Tasmanian Tiger Museum all together? For what kind of factory?"

"Micro-chips."

"And the Northan dynasty supports that does it?"

"The factory will provide employment for people in the town."

"The museum was already providing employment." Wish-Wash turned to Oodles who was standing by the end of his bed holding his towel and clean clothes. "Wasn't it, cobber?" He stared back at the Mayor. "For me. For Oodles. For Moose. For Joffa."

"You two gave it up because it was no longer making money after your latest debacle, and, mark my words, sooner or later Moose and Joffa will end up back in jail. The only surprising thing to me is how they were ever let out in the first place."

Wish-Wash scratched his beard. "Have you thought about Katy now being a partner? Another mouth to feed."

"She can always go back to cutting hair."

"Where? Your daughter has already bought the salon to set up your granddaughters!"

"Vicki and Velda might take her on as a part-time contractor. Or she can set up a business in another town to be closer to Joffa's prison."

Wish-Wash gasped. "You have no respect for tradition, do you?"

"What tradition?" He summoned up the script he had used way back in his holier-than-thou political days. "The Tasmanian Government declared the Tasmanian Tiger extinct in 1986 and even that was way behind the times. The International Union for the Conservation of

Nature called its extinction in 1982 — 46 years after the last-known
Tasmanian Tiger died on a cold night in the Hobart zoo."

It was hard to guess whether Wish-Wash was shivering with cold
or quivering with anger. "Trust a bloody mongrel bastard like you.
People like Moose believe the Tasmanian Tiger is still out there. He's a
true believer. People have seen them, including me."

"I didn't believe you in 1967 and I don't believe you now."

"Other people believed me though. Media came from all over the
country to interview me."

"Fake news before it was even a thing. And it's the reason your
museum ever got a foothold. It caters for gullible fools. What were you
even thinking with your latest attempt to pass off a native cat for a
Tasmanian Tiger?"

"That was a misunderstanding, a bit of bad luck — and you know
it. If Moose hadn't busted his ankle, Joffa and Awesome Sauce
wouldn't have been in well over their heads."

The Mayor wasn't swayed. "We will be much better off without the
museum staining Windy Mountain's reputation. Investors need to
know the town is now open for business."

Wish-Wash shook his head and looked up at Oodles.

Oodles scratched his head. "I know you're angry right now, old
son, which is a good reason not to reply to Moose until you calm down
a bit and think it through."

"How can I think it through? Two quick offers! There must be
something going on Moose isn't telling us about."

"Perhaps your grandson knows something?"

"I doubt it. He's his father's son. Clueless."

"Have you got his email address?"

"Of course. He has one at work."

"Ask him to suss out what's going on."

TWENTY-ONE
FEELING SHEEPISH

OODLES WOKE up when knocking rattled the door. He craned his head and looked around the room but couldn't work out where he was. The clock on the wall didn't lessen his confusion. It was an Elvis Presley-themed clock, only Elvis seemed to be striking a Saturday Night Fever pose with both arms in the air. Light was streaming through the window but it felt like the middle of the night.

It started to make sense when he saw the other two old men had dozed off on their beds, too, and then he remembered everything.

Oodles had dressed into clean clothes after his shower, but the Mayor was lying on his back with a towel around his midriff. Wish-Wash had been fine with him washing out the borrowed socks and underpants in the bathroom basin but he winced when he saw the shirt hanging over the space heater, too.

Wish-Wash was covered with a blanket and was snoring away.

The Mayor was rubbing his eyes. "How can Bert not have heard that?" Just then, more knocking came.

"I reckon that's for you, James." Oodles whispered.

"Me? What makes you think that?"

"The roadside-assist man must have arrived."

"Already? How long have we been asleep."

"Well over two hours."

This hadn't been the plan. They had talked about keeping each other awake for as long as possible to fight off jet-lag.

"You'll have to get the door; I'm not decent," the Mayor said.

"I'm sure Shamus has seen a man with a towel around him before."

The Mayor lowered his voice even further. "No way!"

"For Gawdsake," Oodles said, rising. "I'll go then. If someone doesn't answer it soon ..."

He didn't finish the sentence because right then a lock turned in the door,

This new noise finally caused Wish-Wash to wake with a start, and throw back the blankets. He looked like the kind of flabby man Reubens might have enjoyed painting had he not been fixated with big, buxom women. Shamus's wife Cathleen came through the door.

————

She backed out of the room.

Oodles followed her, apologising.

Turns out Cathleen had been knocking for some time. When no one answered, she feared something might have happened. She carried spare keys in her apron pocket and it seemed the right thing to check it out. She was so sorry though.

"Oh, don't worry, love," Oodles said.

"But yer poor man! Naked!"

"I wouldn't worry about Wish-Wash feeling embarrassed. He has a thick skin. This is not his fault though. All his clean clothes are locked in the car."

Yes, dat's why she was there. The roadside-assist man was downstairs.

"Yes, I figured it was him. Please tell him we'll be down in a jiffy."

Oodles excused himself and went back into the room.

The Mayor was slipping on Lambsie when he came in; Wish-Wash was standing in front of the window stretching and yawning, and baring his all to the outside world.

The Mayor sat down on his bed and bent down to put on his shoes and socks. "Is the roadside-assist man here?"

"He's downstairs waiting."

The Mayor puffed as he twisted a sock on to a foot, and he screwed up his face.

"Still damp?" Oodles asked.

"Not really. The shirt and undies were still damp. I'd call these socks still wringing wet."

Oodles laughed. "Get a wriggle on. Sooner we get the car open, sooner we can get Wish-Wash decent again."

The Mayor said, "Will you come away from that window, Bert? Anyone would think you enjoy flashing?"

The fat adonis turned his head. "Just you close that door behind you. I'll await my luggage."

————

While they watched the roadside-assist man try to open the window with a wire coat hanger Cathleen had given him, Oodles wondered if you could still do that with modern cars.

But the Mayor looked like he had other things on his mind as he patted his pockets.

When he pulled out the keys, he couldn't help to look anything other than sheepish in that jumper. "What do you know? I didn't lock them in the car after all."

TWENTY-TWO
THREE MEN WALK INTO AN IRISH PUB

THE LARGE BARTENDER looked at Wish-Wash through the haze of his cigarette smoke, and smiled. "So, yer the man come to fix up the castle?"

It was almost 1pm but he looked like he had just got out of bed.

His bloodshot eyes matched the colour of his red trousers, his hair looked in serious need of a comb, and he was using an empty shot glass as an ashtray.

The Mayor had alarm on his face when he turned to Oodles and mouthed: "He's smoking!"

Oodles knew what he was on about. It was big news even in Australia when they outlawed smoking in Irish pubs. But Oodles wasn't about to chastise the bartender.

Would you look at him! He might have lacked the dexterity to line up the buttons on his floral shirt, but Oodles didn't doubt he still had the strength to rip someone's head off if he was angered. Wish-Wash was just as big but he'd be giving away 30 years.

The bartender scratched his stubble. "Sorry the place is in a bit of a mess. We was watching a big football international last night. It went a wee bit late."

By the look of it, a substantial section of the village had been in the bar. Oodles's eyes were still adjusting to the light, but now he could make out empty pint glasses and glasses with slops scattered on every available surface — along the bar, low tables, on top of the TV in the corner, even on some of the stools. Some glasses had cigarette butts floating in the dregs.

The bartender sucked on his cigarette and blew out the smoke. "What can I get you fellas?"

"We heard you served a nice lunch here," Wish-Wash said.

"Aye. Maureen's just opened the kitchen." He pointed to a blackboard in the corner. "The lamb is off though."

"How can it be off?" Wish-Wash said loudly. He was often agitated when he was hungry, and it had been hours since his meagre breakfast. "You said she's just opened the flaming kitchen. That would suggest to me we're the first customers of the day."

"You're the first fecking customers of the past *two weeks*," the bartender shouted back. "Dat's why the lamb is off. Maureen took the meat out of the fridge two weeks ago and forgot to put it back in."

Wish-Wash dropped the volume. "Oh!" He was taken aback. "What would you recommend?"

"The seafood chowder is grand. You like purdies?"

Wish-Wash frowned. "Purdies?"

The bartender said it louder. "Purdies." He looked to one of the other men in the bar for linguistic help.

"Potatoes to you." The interpreter who turned around was wearing a black fisherman's beanie and an ill-fitting grey suit, and when the Mayor saw him it looked like he had seen a ghost.

Oodles knew what was going through his mind. So he tapped the Mayor's shin with his walking stick, hard, to distract him.

"Ouch, what did you do that for?" The Mayor bent down and rubbed his shin.

"Sorry, the stick has a life of its own." Oodles turned his attention to the man in the suit. "What if my doctor told me to cut back on potatoes?"

The man flashed an incomplete smile. He had two missing front teeth. He turned back towards the bar and addressed his drinking companions. "Would you be hearing dat? We have a man here who lets his doctor push him around." He swivelled back around and addressed Oodles. "Would you be talking about a certain type of potato? We're very versatile here. You can have dem mashed, boiled, roasted, or cut into french fries."

"What do they come with?" Oodles said.

"The mashed purdies come with boiled purdies, roasted purdies and french fries, and the french fries come with mashed purdies, boiled purdies, and roasted purdies, and the roast purdies come with—"

Wish-Wash broke in. This was testing his patience for food. "But do they come with flaming meat?"

"Aye. Beef or a nice piece of cod. Or they put them in with the seafood chowder."

The bartender took his last drag then screwed his cigarette butt into the shot glass. The glass grew cloudy with the dying puffs of smoke. He nodded towards the man in the suit. "Conn used to be a fisherman on trawlers. There is not much work for him around here now. Pity. Hard to find good workers like him. I expect he'll be one of the first people yer'll want to hire when you start the renovation work on yer castle."

———

A young woman cleared a table for the old men at the back of the room while they were ordering drinks. It was near the open fire glowing in the big stone hearth.

The bartender brightened when Oodles ordered a pint of Guinness, but he looked less pleased when the Mayor asked for a half pint of Belgian lager. When Wish-Wash asked if he could add raspberry syrup to his lemonade, he looked positively disgusted.

The old men all settled on seafood chowder, which came in big bowls with two serves each of soda bread.

"This smells nice." Oodles sniffed in the aroma. "Don't dob on me to Doc Jenko though."

The steaming bowls contained white sauce filled with cod and mussels. And purdies of course.

Wish-Wash needed no encouragement. He got to work slurping.

The Mayor loaded up his spoon, took a sip, then dropped it with a small splash before the crash on the bottom of the china bowl. "I can't believe Mr Potato Head over there is brazen enough to wear my stolen suit in front of me."

"Steady." Oodles pointed his silver spoon at the Mayor. "You can't go accusing people of theft without evidence."

The Mayor tugged at his trouser leg. "Same colour, see. If you want more evidence, take a look at the tag on the inside pocket. You'll find my tailor's name on it."

Oodles studied his face to determine whether he was serious. "And you think that bloke will let you examine the coat? Get real!"

The Mayor looked blankly back at him. "I get it now. That's why you rapped me with your walking stick. It damn-well hurt."

"It was for your own good. If you had tried to make a citizen's arrest, you would have ended up looking foolish."

"We'll see who the fool is and who the smart one is when I find out that ratbag's name and report him to the gardai. They should have never ended transportation from here to the colonies. Nothing but riff-raff!"

"You'd know!" It was the first time Wish-Wash had come up for breath from his shovelling. "What did your great, great, great grandfather do to get seven years?"

"Oh, very droll, Bert." The Mayor picked up a piece of the brown bread and examined it, and let out a deep breath. "Cod has never been my favourite fish. Cakes of soap have more flavour."

"You're joking, aren't you?" Wish-Wash said. "No one ever told me cakes of soap were this delicious."

The Mayor pushed the barely touched bowl away. "I wish I had ordered the beef now."

"You still can, can't he Oodles?" Wish-Wash glanced across the table. "Waste not, want not though. Push the bowl this way."

The Mayor tossed back his head. "Would you jump in my grave as quickly!"

"You'll have to kick the bucket first so you can find out."

"Oh, that's nice, that is? After all I've been through! Is this the thanks I get for paying for all these meals?"

"Do you have to go on?" Oodles said. "We said we'd pay you back. Shamus says banks in Letterkenny will exchange our money."

"We can kill two birds with one stone," Wish-Wash added. "They're expecting me to drop into the regional branch of the company that did the genetic DNA test. You and Oodles can pop in, too."

"Oh, do I have to?" the Mayor groaned. "Seems to me my time would be better spent finding a men's clothing store."

"It won't kill you to say thanks, you know," Wish-Wash said. "They were very good about me stuffing them around with the tickets."

The Mayor exhaled noisily. "All right. If I must." He tapped the wallet in his front pocket. "I'll do my shopping while you're busy in the bank though. I don't even need to change money. My credit card will do me fine. How far away is this Letterbox?"

"Letterkenny!" Oodles corrected him. "Guess we'll find out how far away it is tomorrow."

"Pay more attention to the address you enter in the G.P.S.," the Mayor said. "We don't want to end up in the wrong city again." He turned to Wish-Wash. "And if you think you can con me into funding your *castle* renovations, you have another thing coming."

"You picked up on that, too?" Wish-Wash blew on his spoon, slurped then burped. "It was news to me. I purposely didn't reply."

"It sounded to me like," Oodles said, "they think you're The Great White Hope who's going to boost employment for the village."

"The Great White Dope, more like it," the Mayor said.

Wish-Wash looked daggers at him. "Who's the rude one now?"

"Well, I ask you? Would you mistake a man in a lime green suit as being a member of Mensa."

"At least I'm wearing a fresh shirt and fresh underwear. You're wearing the same clothes you arrived in. What's that say about you?"

"I washed them! You saw them drying, Oodles, didn't you?"

"You didn't wash Lambsie," Wish-Wash said. "That jumper was made from the finest Peruvian wool but it now smells like dags swept out from the shearing-shed floor."

"Peru? You don't think they saw you coming in the shop?" The Mayor's voice grew progressively louder. "That it really is made out of dags and the nearest it's been to South America was South Oatlands?"

"You ungrateful turd!"

"You think I like wearing this?" The Mayor trembled with rage. "You think I like looking like an ageing hippy? I didn't ask the airline to lose my luggage! I didn't ask for my suitcase to be pillaged up at the castle!"

Wish-Wash looked at Oodles. "Christ Almighty, anyone would think it's my fault."

"You can understand James's frustration," Oodles said. "The question is: what are you going to do about this castle malarkey?"

Wish-Wash had started on his second helping. His loaded spoon teetered over the bowl. "What can I do but keep my ear close to the ground to try to suss out what's happening? I'm still trying to work out how he even knew I was the new owner of the castle."

"Probably an educated guess, old son," Oodles said. "He obviously knew when we were arriving and he picked up on the Aussie accents as soon as we walked in."

———

The bartender walked over and put another log on the fire. He prodded the embers with a poker, and the new log crackled and hissed before catching fire. The red and purple became enlivened with yellow flames.

He stood and looked at it for a moment, then turned, looked at his watch and took two strides towards the old men's table. "We still have a couple of hours of daylight left. I was thinking. We want to give you a good welcome up at the castle."

"When? Now?" Wish-Wash said.

"Naw, in about half an hour. You fellas have a car? Don't worry about bringing a ting. Just get yerselves up there."

The Mayor pointed to the man in the grey suit over at the bar and hissed: "Will he be there?"

The bartender followed the direction of his finger. "Conn? Yer'll be wanting an experienced builder like Conn."

"I thought you said he was a fisherman?" Oodles said.

"Aye, that, too. Carpenter, butcher, stone mason . . . there's not much Conn Northan can't turn his hand to."

The Mayor spluttered. "What did you call him?"

"Conn Northan. Why? Do you tink you know him?"

The Mayor spread his arms out on the table and buried his head. "It's getting worse," came his muffled voice.

The bartender looked down. "What's wrong with him?"

"I think he just discovered a long lost relative," Oodles said.

"Him, too?" The barman stretched out his hand to Wish-Wash. "I oughta have introduced myself when you arrived. I'm Malachy Willson, yer distant cousin. I'm the one who sent you the email, congratulating you for inheriting the castle. I tought I was next in line for it, but fair's fair."

TWENTY-THREE
SMILE!

THEY HAD time to go back to the B&B to freshen up before going up to the castle.

Cathleen stopped the vacuum cleaner when they entered the reception area.

"You've been to the pub for lunch? How was Malachy?"

"He had had a big night."

Cathleen shook her head. "He's always recovering from a big night. He's a bad influence on Shamus, he is. He'd be lost without Maureen and Katy, he would."

"His kitchen staff?"

"His wife and daughter. Maureen does the cooking, Katy works front of house."

Oodles pointed to Wish-Wash. "Turns out he's related to Bert here."

"Oh aye. I wouldn't shout that too loudly. The gards might hear." She eyed the hoover. "I better get back to it. Do me a favour though. If you see my weans, tell them I'm looking for them."

"Your weans?" Oodles said.

"Donal and Mary."

"Your husband didn't call them weans."

"Naw. He wouldn't. He's from Dublin. He still calls them chiselers. Actually, he's been calling them a lot worse since they found dat dog. Heaven knows where it came from? I know every one of the two hundred or so people in this village and none of them has a new dog as far as I know."

"If we see them, we'll let you know," Oodles said, and the three old men went on their way.

Oodles brought up the rear as they climbed the stairs, and Wish-Wash turned his head. "I never took you as a dobber, cobber."

Oodles stopped mid-step and put his weight on to his walking stick. "What makes you say that?"

When they heard quickening footsteps ahead of them, Wish-Wash turned his head to see Lambsie disappearing around the corner at the top of the stairs. "The bugger's only rushing to be first in the bathroom."

Oodles grabbed him by the tail of his shirt as he flexed to give chase. "Let him have a little win, old son. Otherwise he'll lose heart. This is a long trip. You'll have lots of other opportunities to humiliate him."

Wish-Wash's face dropped. "I guess you're right."

They resumed walking up slowly.

"Besides," Oodles said, two steps later. "It'll give you time to check the email, and to find your new glasses."

Wish-Wash stopped and turned around again, causing Oodles to almost run into the back of him.

"I've told you before. I don't even need those glasses."

"Doc Jenkins reckons you do. So does Goody."

"They're not here."

Oodles looked up into his face. "You didn't even bring them, did you?"

"Of course I brought them. I told you: they're in my suitcase."

"Why would you even bring them if you reckon you don't need them?"

"I knew I'd never hear the end of it from you if I didn't. First you want to give up those poor kids even though they've done nothing to you, next you'll report back to Jenko about me." He raised his hand repeatedly like a goody-goody-two-shoes schoolboy eager to tell on a classmate. "*Sir, sir. Wish-Wash left his glasses at home, sir.*"

Oodles shook his head. "I've got no intention of squealing on those kids. I was just trying to appease Cathleen after her nasty shock. And I've got no intention of dobbing you into Doc Jenkins. If you want to be blind as a bat that's up to you."

Wish-Wash must have felt shamed because almost the first thing he did back in the room was produce his red glasses case.

"So you've decided to wear them up at the castle, old son?"

Wish-Wash snapped the case shut. "I didn't say that."

———

Wish-Wash said he didn't want people he knew to see him like that.

"No one here knows you!" Oodles said.

"It's not the people here I'm worried about."

Those cryptic words were still ringing in Oodles's ears when he drove the car down the hill, changing down through the gears.

Malachy Willson had brought dozens of people with him and they were unloading plastic chairs and tables from the back of a truck, and were laying the tables out with glasses and plates of food.

Oodles raised his hand to them as the car idled past.

He parked about 25 yards up from the castle.

"It looks like they plan to feed the Great White Hope," he quipped as the old men walked towards the castle.

Wish-Wash rubbed his belly. "Oh, I'm counting on it."

"You just ate, old son!"

"It'd be rude to not eat what they are offering."

It was around 3.30pm. The sun had never really gathered enough heat together to pretend the day was warm, but there were patches of blue between the clouds.

Both Oodles and Wish-Wash had rugged up a bit more. Oodles had changed into his favourite overalls under his duffle coat, Wish-Wash had pulled out a yellow jumper to wear with his lime green suit, the Mayor had Lambsie to keep him warm.

When they reached the fringe of the activity, the Mayor sniffed the air. "Mmm. Smells like Irish stew. Yum."

He was wrong. What they were ladling into bowls was seafood chowder.

Malachy, now rugged up in a jumper that consisted of red, green and yellow triangles knitted together, winked at him as he went to hand him a bowl. "Ye can't get too much of this."

The Mayor raised a palm. "Oh, I couldn't eat another thing."

Malarchy frowned. "Would you like a pint?" He pointed with his other hand to where Katy was filling glasses. "Help yerself to a Guinness over there."

The Mayor raised his palm again. "I'm fine, really."

Wish-Wash stepped past him. "Can I have his, cousin?"

"Of course. The guest of honour can have what he wants." He nodded to the front table, where Conn Northan was already sitting with a man with their back to them. Conn was still dressed in that grey suit and was wiping Guinness froth from his mouth.

"I'm not sitting there," the Mayor said.

Malachy frowned. "I thought you'd want to sit with yer relative? It'd give you a chance to catch up, find some common ground."

The Mayor blinked slowly. "I'll just grab a lemonade from the drinks table and sit at one of the tables near the back."

Malachy shrugged. "Please yerself."

"Don't worry, he normally does please himself," Wish-Wash said as they watched the back of the Mayor disappearing. He sat down on the fixed park bench at the back of the gathering.

"Dat so? It must run in the family. Good man, Conn. But he has a mind of his own." Malachy shook his head. "I expect you can't wait to tell us when the restoration work on the castle will start."

"Give us a break," Wish-Wash said. "I need a few days to acclimatise. Jet-lag!"

"Of course. Take all the time you need." Malachy looked up at the tower. "The castle isn't going anywhere. Nor is yer workforce. Sit yourselves down, both of you." He looked at Oodles with his walking stick. "I'll get the girls to bring yer food over."

When Oodles and Wish-Wash went to the table, and sat down next to each other, they saw immediately the man who had his back to them was Shamus, from the B&B. What's more, he was wearing a grey suit identical to the one Conn Northan was wearing. Good thing the Mayor wasn't at the same table. He would have had an apoplexy.

Conn Northan extended a hand. Oodles might have known it'd be like shaking a lukewarm teabag. Some mannerisms are enshrined in the DNA, and he had shaken the Mayor's hand often enough.

"Conn Northan reporting for duty." The Irishman looked up at the tower. "If the weather is kind to us, we oughta have it done by the tourist season."

Malachy had followed them to the table, and sat down at the end, just as the waitresses were delivering pints of Guinness. "You already know Shamus?"

"Yes," Wish-Wash said.

The owner of the B&B nodded. "So did you lay eyes on my chiselers?"

Oodles shook his head.

"If I find out where they're hiding dat fecking dog ..."

Oodles looked sideways at Wish-Wash who was running a finger down the outside of his pint glass. "Do you want me to tell them?" he whispered.

"Tell them what?"

"Tell them you don't actually drink any more."

Wish-Wash shook his head. "Not yet. I need this as a prop for the photo."

"What photo?"

Right then, Malachy stood up and raised his glass. "I propose a toast. Cousin Bert tells me there's work here for whoever wants it."

Much cheering erupted and Wish-Wash and Oodles looked at each other. Oodles knew Wish-Wash had said no such thing. When had he even had the chance?

But they smiled politely when Malachy sat down, just as two pretty young women placed steaming bowls in front of them.

"Will you do me a favour, cuz?" Wish-Wash said. "Got a phone camera, have you? I want the folks back at home to share this moment. Would you mind?"

"Not at all."

"Can we get the girls in the picture, too?"

"Aye. Grand." He called after the waitresses. When they turned, he beckoned them back with his finger. "Katy, you sit on uncle Bert's knee. Philomena, you sit on the other ol' one's lap." He turned and looked the Mayor's way. "Does he want to be in the photo, too?"

"No, he'd probably only break your camera with the face he's pulling," Wish-Wash said.

"Sure? The girl I'd put on his knee might cheer him up. He's not to know Riona Northan is a blood relative."

"No, leave him out of it," Wish-Wash said. "He'll have enough excitement tomorrow. We're going to Letterkenny."

"And why's dat?"

"Oodles and I need to change some money; Jimbo needs to buy some new clothes."

Malachy looked towards the Mayor again. "What's wrong with the clothes he's got on? Dat's a very fetching sweater."

"I think so, too." Wish-Wash beamed. "I lent it to him after his suit-case went missing."

Oodles noticed Malachy exchange quick glances with Conn and Shamus.

Malachy stood up and reached inside his jumper to extract his phone. "I'd better take this photo before we lose good light."

———

Malachy later emailed the photo to Wish-Wash. It showed Oodles and Wish-Wash nursing pints of Guinness and village girls on their laps. The Mayor was in the background nursing a lemonade, and with a look on his face that suggested that the village might have run out of good-looking young sheilas.

Oodles watched Wish-Wash reattach it to an email destined for home. "Aren't you going to tell them the truth behind the photo? Or at least that pint in front of you? They'll think you've fallen off the wagon?"

"Let them think what they like?" Wish-Wash said. "Moose has told me bugger-all about what's happening to trigger not one but two offers for the museum. Let him be jealous, I say."

"You're not going to tell him that young woman was actually a relative?"

"I'm not going to say she isn't!"

Oodles puffed out his cheeks. "Nothing has come back from young Rod?"

"Not yet. But give him a chance? With the time difference, he's probably still asleep."

TWENTY-FOUR
SNAKE!

THE MAYOR DECIDED 10pm would be a good time to ring his lawyer at home, so he filled in time looking at his phone while the others read. He forced himself to peruse the Windy Mountain newspaper, *The Pick of the Crop*, online. Oodles knew the reason for his reluctance about reading it was twofold.

One: it wasn't his beloved *Financial Review*.

Two: he didn't see eye to eye with the bloke who ran the hick paper, who happened to be his son-in-law, Norm Hit, who had married way above his station.

At 9.45pm, the Mayor let out a yelp.

Oodles looked up from his e-reader. "What's the matter, old son? Something bite you?"

James Northan prodded his phone. "Cedric was only 46. My lawyer has died."

———

That night Oodles was awakened when Wish-Wash rolled out of bed and tip-toed towards the door.

"Where are you going, old son?" he whispered.

"I can't sleep so I'm going to make myself a cup of tea downstairs."

"At this time of night!" Oodles raised himself up from his pillow. "The caffeine in tea's not going to help you to sleep."

"Everything is opposite on this side of the world. Haven't you seen the way the water swirls backwards down the plughole?" Wish-Wash slammed the door behind him.

This noise woke James Northan up. "What! What's going on?" he spluttered.

"Nothing to worry about, old son," Oodles said. "Wish-Wash says he can't sleep."

"So he's woken everyone up? Typical!"

"He's just gone downstairs to make himself a cup of tea."

The Mayor turned on his bedside lamp and blinked at his Rolex. "It's past 2am, for goodness sake! How are we going to get on the road early if Bert keeps us up all night?"

"He'll be awake early enough. You ever know Wish-Wash to miss breakfast?"

The Mayor rolled back on to his stomach and reached up and clicked off his lamp. "What's the bet I'll just be dozing off again when the clodhopper bursts back through the door?"

It was quicker than he expected.

Wish-Wash was back within a minute, and switched on the main light.

Oodles shielded his eyes with his hands. "Did you have to do that?"

"For goodness sake," the Mayor said.

"I have to send an email."

Oodles sat up in bed again. "Strewth! What's so urgent?"

"There's something in the kitchen."

"No kidding!" Oodles said. "It's a kitchen. There are probably lots of things in there. Kettle, microwave, toaster, tea bags …"

"Things that move?"

"Move?" Oodles stared at him.

"There's something moving in one the cupboard under the sink."

"What is it?" Oodles narrowed his eyes.

"How do I know?"

"Didn't you open the cupboard to look?"

"No! When I heard the rustling, my first thought was to get out of there."

"Strewth, old son! Have you ever thought it might have just been a mouse?"

Wish-Wash shook his head. "It sounded a lot bigger than a mouse to me. If you ask me, it's a snake."

The Mayor raised his head to the light. "You fool. There are no snakes in Ireland."

"How do you know?"

"Everyone knows St Patrick chased all the snakes out of Ireland."

Wish-Wash put his hands on his hips. "And you reckon I'm gullible! How's one man supposed to have gotten every single snake? Obviously, he missed the one hiding in the kitchen cupboard!"

The Mayor fell back into his pillow face-first and punched the side. "Spare me!"

"I'm going to email Moose and ask what he recommends."

"Believe me, he's just going to laugh at you," the muffled voice said.

"I doubt that. The main person he laughs at is you."

The Mayor lifted his head again and gave a searing look.

"Anyway, " Wish-Wash said. "That's why I had to turn on the light. I have to look for my laptop."

"*My* laptop, you mean?"

"No, the one the airline gave me."

"Couldn't you have located it in the dark?"

"I can't remember where I hid it."

"See, that's proof it's my computer; why else would you have hidden it?"

"General security." Wish-Wash put his hand to his head gleefully. "I remember now." He walked over to the Mayor's bed, bent down, and slid the laptop out.

"You hid it under my bed?"

"Clever, eh?" *Hee-haw, hee-haw.* "You didn't think of looking there."

The Mayor sank into his pillow again. "Just send your email and switch off the light when you're finished. Don't forget we're off to Letterkenny first thing."

TWENTY-FIVE
DICK!

As Oodles had predicted, Wish-Wash had no trouble rousing them at 6.30am. Half an hour later, he was leading the two other old men down the stairs with a spring in his step.

Cathleen delivered three full Irish breakfasts to their table — eggs, bacon, baked beans, black pudding and soda bread. It was all a bit much for two of the bleary-eyed elderly zombies.

Only Wish-Wash stepped up to the plates to help the others out.

You had to hand it to him. The big bloke was resilient. He was amazingly cheerful given the circumstances. Anyone else might have wilted in the face of the tirade of abuse he got for keeping them awake so long.

He had taken almost an hour to one-finger tap out his email.

Worse, he had mumbled to himself while he was doing it, too.

He did eventually turn off the light. It was probably the only time in history someone had been clapped for doing this. The one reason he didn't get a standing ovation was it was so cold and Oodles and the Mayor were snuggled under their quilts.

———

They all decided to have a nap after breakfast.

Wish-Wash set an alarm to go off in an hour's time.

The problem was he set it on the laptop, which he proceeded to hide somewhere in a place that must have been soundproof.

It was lunchtime by the time Oodles woke up and realised the others were still snoring.

———

Wish-Wash said he couldn't possibly travel until he had eaten.

"Are you kidding me?" the Mayor said. "We just ate. If you want to add up all the bacon you ate, your own black pudding, the black pudding I gave you from my plate, and the black pudding Oodles gave you, you've probably eaten the good part of a pig."

"You make it sound like I gorged myself on unhealthy food. You forget I ate everyone's baked beans, too! "

"Don't I know it! Now we're going to have to keep the windows open all the way to Letterkenny!"

"What are you saying?"

The Mayor looked to Oodles for support. "James has a point, old cock. It's cold enough without having to open the windows."

"I still need to eat before the drive."

The Mayor raised his wrist and tapped on his watch. "Can't you grab a takeaway to eat in the car. Time is really getting on."

"What's the hurry?" Wish-Wash said.

"Isn't it obvious? We don't even know what time the bank closes!"

Wish-Wash looked at Oodles. "That's not quite true, is it cobber?"

"No, 4 o'clock is what I was told," Oodles said. "For most of the branches anyway."

"Oh? Who told you that?" the Mayor said.

"Your cousin Conn," Wish-Wash said. "You would have heard it, too, if you had sat where they wanted you to sit yesterday."

The Mayor rolled his eyes. "You believed him, did you? You don't think the name Conn might be short for Conman?"

"That's a terrible thing to say about your own flesh and blood, Jimbo?" Wish-Wash snarled.

"That's you making an assumption! Just because he has the same surname, does not mean he is related."

"You're joking! He even looks like a younger version of you. What's more, DNA genetic testing proved this is the area *Colonel* Richard Northan came from. He's your great, great, great grandfather, remember?"

"I'm not denying that. But we know this Conn Northan is a common thief. I caught him red-handed wearing one of my suits."

"That reminds me," Wish-Wash said. "You know who else we saw wearing the other suit you brought in that suitcase?"

The Mayor's eyes widened. "Who?" he spluttered. "Where … when?"

Wish-Wash stroked his beard, slowly, like he was deliberately trying to keep the Mayor in suspense. "You would have seen him for yourself if you had been sitting at the right table up at the castle."

"Why would I have wanted to make eye-contact with anyone at that table?" the Mayor hissed.

"If you had been looking you would have seen Shamus dressed up as you, too." Wish-Wash grinned at him. Or was he baring his teeth like a donkey?

"Shamus? From here at the B&B?"

"Same bloke. He was even wearing one of your blue ties." *Hee-haw, hee-haw.*

The Mayor raked his hair. "Oh, this is the dizzy limit." He lowered his voice. "Is everyone on the take in this godforsaken town?"

"I guess they have tradition to live up to. What did you say your great, great, great grandfather did to get shipped out as a convict to Van Diemen's Land?" Wish-Wash gave him the equine grin again.

"It was so long ago, I don't even care." At this, the Mayor reached up and switched off his hearing aids and stormed off into the bathroom.

It was Oodles's turn to grin at Wish-Wash. "You certainly know how to yank his chain."

"I'm only starting," Wish-Wash said. "He cares, all right. And I'm going to find out." He shifted his facial expression. "We have time to eat before we go to Letterkenny, don't we?"

Oodles looked at his watch. "I suppose so. Conn reckoned it's an easy hour's drive. He gave me directions."

"You understood everything he was saying?"

"Not really. I'll just follow the signs. How hard could it be?"

———

Malachy Willson was surprised when they walked into the pub. "I tought you fellas were going to Letterkenny this morning?"

"Dat's what I tought, too," the man in the grey suit nursing a pint at the bar said. "Did you get lost?"

The Mayor took one look at Conn Northan and kept walking to the table furtherest away, over near the fire again. Oodles and Wish-Wash didn't move from the plush red carpet in front of the bar. Conn was wearing the grey suit again and Malachy was wearing the same floral shirt as yesterday. Oodles had put on fresh overalls and Wish-Wash had broken out his stretchy green and orange trackie-dackies with an almost matching swirly purple and puce jumper.

Conn Northan watched the Mayor walking away and lowered his voice. "He doesn't like me, does he?"

"I wouldn't take it to heart, old son," Oodles said. "James doesn't like most people."

Wish-Wash seized his chance. "You know you two are related?"

"Aye. Malachy told me. Dat's what makes it a bit hurtful. We ought to be bonding. The way I figure it, my great, great, great, great grandfather must have been his great, great, great grandfather."

Wish-Wash brightened. "You know about Richard Northan then?"

"Of course. The story has been handed down in the family. It was a dark day indeed when Dick Northan was sentenced to seven years as a convict. They knew he was never coming back from a colony on the other side of the world."

"What did you call him?" Wish-Wash said.

"Dick. Dat's what everyone called him. Big Dick. But dat was probably ironic, like. He was a wee man so what were the chances?"

"Do you know what he was transported for?"

"Aye. He stole three purdies."

"Potatoes? Seven years for stealing three potatoes!"

"It's where he dug them up from that caused him grief. Purdies were hard to come by in those days but there was a nice dry vegetable patch up at the castle." He pointed to Malachy. "But you didn't steal from Paddy Willson and get away with it."

Oodles looked alternatively at the men on either side of the bar. "But you two have buried the hatchet?"

"Aye," Malachy said. "Dat's why I'm so keen for you to hire Conn. It will complete the healing process." He let that hang there, then said, "When do you tink you'll want to start?"

———

Oodles took a long pull of his half-pint, then licked his lips. "When are you going to tell him, old son?"

Wish-Wash and Oodles had joined the Mayor at the table in the corner. The fire was roaring and warm. Oodles had opted for a small Guinness, since he'd soon be driving, and Wish-Wash and the Mayor both had glasses of lemonade. They had ordered their meals — more seafood chowder for Oodles and Wish-Wash, the Mayor had gone for the Irish stew.

"Tell who what?" Wish-Wash said.

"Your cousin," Oodles said. "You need to stop stringing him along about renovating the castle."

"Oh, that? I thought you might be asking when I was going to tell Jimbo why Grandfather Dick got transported."

The Mayor slammed his fist on the table and the cutlery jumped.

"How dare you call him by that name! He was never called Dick. I told Moose just before he assaulted me with that trophy, and now I'm telling you." *Bang.* "Richard." *Bang.* "Richard." *Bang.* "Richard." *Bang.* "Get it!"

Wish-Wash put his knife and fork back in place. "Conn begs to differ."

"You weren't actually speaking to that reprobate?"

"He wants to know why his cousin refuses to bond with him."

"I told you before: there is no actual evidence he's even my cousin."

"How come you share a common ancestor?"

"He would say that. He wants to weasel his way into an inheritance."

"He actually spoke very highly of Big Dick."

The Mayor's red face looked ready to explode.

"It's me who should be angry," Wish-Wash said. "You want to know what he did to get transported?"

"I certainly do not. I told you, I don't even care."

Wish-Wash was too quick for him this time. No sooner had the Mayor switched off his hearing aids, the big man reached across the table and switched them on again.

"You need to hear this, Jimbo. You might have hoped he had committed some highfaluting crime like embezzlement — but the truth is he was caught stealing potatoes." Wish-Wash held up three fingers. "Three purdies." He held up four more fingers on his other hand. "For which he was given seven years' hard labour in the colonies."

The Mayor shifted awkwardly in his chair. "That's ridiculous."

"Oh, is it? Well, I've got a bone to pick with you. You know where he nicked the purdies from?" Wish-Wash prodded his own chest. "Only from my great, great, great grandfather's garden."

The Mayor closed his eyes.

"I'd say you owe me, Jimbo. My family never got those potatoes back."

Oodles knew Wish-Wash had made that last bit up but it had the desired effect.

The Mayor said nothing until he took the first mouthful of his Irish stew, which he promptly spat back on to the plate. "Yuk! I think this stew might be made from the same lamb that was off yesterday."

"Good thing you weren't hungry, Jimbo," Wish-Wash said between slurps of his seafood chowder. "But if you get peckish in the car just yell and we'll look for a McDonald's drive-through."

Oodles looked down at the soda bread on his side-plate, and sighed. "I'm not sure I can eat these either. I think that's what's giving me indigestion."

Wish-Wash reached across and grabbed the two pieces of bread. "Don't say I never do things for you."

TWENTY-SIX

'SOMEDAY, SOMEONE'S GOING TO KNOCK THAT SMIRK RIGHT OFF YOUR FACE, LAMBSIE.'

IF WISH-WASH'S stomach even gurgled, Oodles couldn't hear it over the sound of the engine.

So Oodles kept the heater on, and the windows closed.

He chose not to turn on the G.P.S. this time but rely on road signs and the map to direct them to Letterkenny.

Many of the signs were bilingual — Gaelic on the top, English on the bottom — but whoever put them up might have had trouble determining left from right or, perhaps wanted everyone to take the scenic route. They certainly did pass by some lovely green countryside and drove through some quaint villages.

"I'm not sure we're going the right way," came the voice from the back. The rustle of paper told Oodles that the Mayor was re-angling the map.

"I'm just following the blinking signs," Oodles said.

"I saw them, too," Wish-Wash said.

Oodles groaned softly.

Wish-Wash looked sideways. "What's that supposed to mean? I'm on your side, cobber."

"With respect, old son, I still can't work out why you're still not wearing your new glasses."

"I've got by without specs for 83 years, haven't I? How would you like it if the quack made you wear glasses you didn't actually need?"

"That's the point you're missing. You *do* need them. Goody wouldn't have prescribed them otherwise."

The Mayor's voice came from the back. "I don't know why you didn't let me sit in the front this time, Bert? Clarence wouldn't have given me this map if he didn't think I'd be a much better navigator."

Wish-Wash turned around and waved a finger. "I'm a wake-up to you, Jimbo," he said louder than anyone should be allowed to talk in a car with all the windows up. "You'd say anything to get an upgrade. Just be thankful you only have to share the back seat with Oodles's walking stick this time. I only have to snap my fingers and Oodles will turn the car around so we can get the suitcases."

"As if?" the Mayor said. "If we get any further behind schedule, the bank in Letterkenny will be closed. And who will that inconvenience most?" He patted his pocket that showed an indentation of his wallet. "I've got my credit card."

"Someday, someone's going to knock that smirk right off your face, Lambsie."

"You never stop, do you?"

"Nu-uh. Not until you return those potatoes to my family."

"Not this again! Has it occurred to you that that scallywag's relative and my relative were two separate people? Please! Richard Northan might not have been the gallant chap we all believed him to be for so long but do you really think someone in my family would be so grubby?"

Wish-Wash kept looking around. "I think it fits your profile perfectly."

"You can't even prove I'm related to that … that … conman."

"Wanna bet?"

"How?"

Wish-Wash took a long breath, then let it out slowly. "That's for me to know and for you to find out."

TWENTY-SEVEN
'YOU WOULDN'T?'

THEY HIT the outskirts of Letterkenny just before 4pm. So did a lot of other cars — though most of them were coming from the other direction.

It wasn't just cold, it was suddenly dark and wet. The car's wipers were furiously swishing rain and sleet away from the middle of the windscreen.

"I don't know how you can see where you're going?" Wish-Wash said.

"Strewth! That's another reason you ought to be wearing your glasses," Oodles said.

"I'd need night-vision goggles when it's this wintry."

"That reminds me." Oodles switched on the headlights. If anything, the light bouncing off sheets of rain made visibility even poorer.

He hit the brakes at a roundabout and the car skidded to a stop.

In front of him, a steady line of cars continued around the roundabout.

Wish-Wash waved his hands. "Why did you stop? We'll never get a break in the traffic now."

"They've got to stop sometime, old son."

Wish-Wash squinted straight ahead and grumbled. "It looks like they're all going into a supermarket. Can't they wait till they get home before they go shopping?"

"Really, Bert," came the voice from the rear seat. "Just because you're in Ireland is no reason to embrace Irish logic." Oodles saw him in the rear-vision mirror look at his watch. "Have either of you gents noticed the time? The bank will be closed before we get there."

"Hmm, I think one branch is open to 4.30pm," Oodles said.

"And you know where this branch is, do you?" the Mayor said.

"No. But you're the one with the map — direct me to the city centre. It's sure to be there somewhere."

Oodles was right about a break occurring in the traffic sooner or later.

But by the sound of some of the honking horns behind them, some people thought Oodles should have bullied his way across sooner.

He held his nerve for a good 10 minutes though, which gave the Mayor time to work out on the map where they were and where they needed to go.

Ten minutes later, they were circling the drenched CDB looking for a parking spot. They weren't the only ones. Cars were circling like sharks and the task wasn't made any easier by the reflections thrown up from water on the bitumen, and the brollies with legs that dashed across the road in front of them.

"Are you sure this is it?" Wish-Wash turned towards the back.

"According to the map, it is," the Mayor said.

"You'd better not make us miss the bank," Wish-Wash said.

"You're trying to blame *me*!" He made himself sound like a Bee Gee hitting a falsetto high. "I'm not the one who kept us all awake half the night, the one who failed to set the alarm properly, or the one who insisted he couldn't travel on an empty stomach!"

Oodles slid the car into a parking spot. "Will you blokes stop bickering." He turned off the engine then looked through the rain-lashed windows. He hadn't seen this much water since he was last in a drive-through car wash. "Which way, James?"

The Mayor tossed his head back. "I don't even know the name of the bank."

"Christ Almighty! This is where you said to come," Wish-Wash said.

"The only request Oodles made was for me to direct him into the city." The Mayor opened his door, which brought the noise of the downpour inside. "Now if you don't mind," he shouted as he grabbed the handle to step down, "I need to find a menswear shop."

"Not so fast," Wish-Wash shouted back.

The Mayor had one leg out of the car, but turned. "What now?" He pulled in his rain-splattered leg, but kept the door ajar.

"You need to find an umbrella shop first," Wish-Wash said.

The Mayor looked out at the water running down the gutter. "I'll make a run for it. It's dry under the awnings."

"I was more worried about Oodles and me," Wish-Wash said. "We don't want to get wet." He looked towards Oodles. "Do we, cobber?"

The Mayor protested. "I can't stop the rain."

"No, but you can go buy us a brolly, Lambsie."

"What?"

"You heard me," Wish-Wash said. "You were the one who wanted to come on this trip — *and* you agreed to carry the bags."

"I never promised to buy any umbrellas!"

"No, but we never foresaw this weather."

Oodles looked at the rain bouncing off the bonnet. The water continued to wash over the windows. He turned his head towards the back. "Wish-Wash has a point, James."

"Ganging up on me, eh?" The Mayor put his leg out the door again. "I'm not going to give in to your bullying this time. Get your own umbrella! You can't make me get you one."

"You're right," Wish-Wash said. "We can't *make* you. But what we *can* do if you don't bring us an umbrella in, say 15 minutes, is move the car to another street."

The Mayor went pale as he retracted his leg again. "You wouldn't?"

"We bloody-well would."

"Even you wouldn't leave me stranded here, Bert."

"I'd like to be a fly on the wall when you finally get back to the B&B, only to find we've checked out and taken your air-ticket with us. Got enough left on your credit card to pay for a trip home?"

"You wouldn't dare," the Mayor hissed. He retracted his leg again and closed the door.

"Oh, I wouldn't worry. They probably have a nice detention centre in Ireland for people who overstay their visas. I'd like to see how your connections go getting you out of trouble this time though."

"People in Windy Mountain would have your guts for garters if you went home without me."

"Are you sure about that? Moose, for one, would probably throw a party. And I doubt Joffa and Katy would lose much sleep. In fact, I can think of about 100 people who'd be *very* happy. And they're just the people still alive. Folks buried in the Windy Mountain graveyard would probably rise from the dead and dance."

"This is extortion," the Mayor hissed.

"Call it what you will," Wish-Wash said. "We're just asking you to fulfil your obligations."

The Mayor slammed the door behind him and Oodles and Wish-Wash watched him scurry for shelter.

"Looks like you've called his bluff," Oodles said.

"Bluff, be buggered. I was serious about moving the car."

"I know you were," Oodles said. "But I'm the one driving and I'd never actually do it."

Wish-Wash studied his face. "Even after the things he's done to you over the years?"

Oodles blew out his cheeks. "I haven't suffered at his hands as much as you. You're right though. A lot of people in Windy Mountain would be mightily pleased if he didn't come back. But Maddie Northan could make our lives hell. I wouldn't be able to drive down the High Street without Sergeant Stretch pulling me up and issuing an infringement ticket. Besides, this parking spot was hard enough to find."

"I think you've gone soft in your old age, cobber. You might feel differently if he's not back within 15 minutes."

Oodles tapped three times on the steering wheel. "You do know we've already missed the bank?"

———

"What do you mean I can't go shopping for clothes now?" The Mayor had wet hair when he returned 14 minutes later with two umbrellas — a small customary black one for him and a large technicolour one for Oodles and Wish-Wash to share.

"It's not my fault the bank has already closed," Wish-Wash said as he inspected the bundled-up umbrella the Mayor had handed to him. "Hey, how did you know red, green, blue, yellow, orange, pink and purple were among my favourite colours?"

"Are they?" the Mayor said, sounding amazed. "Now I know where the shop is, I can take it back?"

"Not on your life." Wish-Wash looked over at Oodles. "You're happy with this one, too, cobber?"

"Doesn't matter what colour it is, old son, as long as it keeps us dry." Actually, this wasn't true. But Oodles knew no one knew him in Letterkenny so would think no less of him when they saw him sheltering under a rainbow-coloured umbrella.

The Mayor had no doubt bought it because he hoped Wish-Wash would hate it as much as the Mayor hated the pink socks, the underpants with the yellow ducks, the shirt with the pineapples, the-dyed jumper, and the Where's Wally beanie. But why would he think that? He really was slipping. Not everyone stuck to dark hues. Wish-Wash was the human kaleidoscope. He hadn't met a bright colour he didn't like.

Wish-Wash spoke sternly. "You're going to have to stick close to us, Jimbo, because I'm the only one with the address, and you won't want to get lost in the crowd."

"I still don't understand why I have to come at all?"

"They're expecting us at the DNA office."

The Mayor looked down at his yellow, red and green tie-dyed jumper. "I can't possibly go there like this! I look like a sheep who's taken LSD. You gents might feel comfortable in footy beanies but I feel downright silly."

"Nonsense. They'll just think we're exotic visitors." Wish-Wash pinched the leg of his green and swirly orange tracksuit pants. "I bet they've never seen the like of these in Letterkenny." Then he looked across to Oodles in his grey overalls and red, white and black beanie. "Your hat could with a few more premierships, cobber, and you could do with a splash more colour. Good reason for you to hold the umbrella."

"No need, old son. Look." Oodles nodded towards the bonnet, which now had a glint from the sun. "The rain has stopped."

TWENTY-EIGHT
'JUST PAY THE MAN, EH?'

THE OFFICE WAS three blocks away, and Wish-Wash carried the umbrella just in case the icy rain returned.

The sign at the door said the DNA genetic office was up a flight of stairs, above a shoe shop.

They stood at the entrance pontificating.

"Why don't you two go up first, and I'll be along soon," the Mayor said.

Wish-Wash shook his head. "How do we know you'll even front?"

"I'm a man of my word, aren't I? I just want to go check out that menswear store we passed, see what they have in my size."

"Can't it wait?" Wish-Wash said.

"Trust me. I've had a lifetime in corporate circles. They'll appreciate seeing one of us wearing a suit and tie."

"What's that supposed to mean? Oodles and I aren't good enough for them — but you are?"

"I didn't say that."

Wish-Wash reached out and plucked from the jumper a strand of wool, which he held up to the light and examined. "If these clever scientists worked out we come from Donegal, I bet they can prove Lambsie really does come from Peru."

The Mayor slapped the strand of wool out of his hand. "Don't be ridiculous, Bert."

"Are you ashamed of Lambsie?"

"I think the word is *allergic*. This jumper gives me sinus. It makes me feel itchy. Passers-by snigger at me. I feel like a character in *The Loudness of the Lambs*."

"There's no such book."

"I might have to write it if I ever get my laptop back."

Wish-Wash looked at him deadpan. "Where is it?"

The Mayor's eyes became little beady reptile eyes. "You know fine-well where it is, Bert."

"Are you accusing me again?"

"I wish I had never agreed to come on this trip. It's been the holiday from hell. As if the flight in cattle-class wasn't awful enough, now I'm reduced to looking like a pantomime sheep. And now you won't let me go and buy some decent clothes."

"Winge, winge, winge," Wish-Wash said. "Anyone would think you're the only one with problems. Let me remind you Oodles and me are still penny-less since we missed the bank."

"And whose fault is that?"

Wish-Wash glared down at him. "You're coming upstairs whether you like it or not."

The Mayor looked down at his fleece of many colours. "Like this? I'd be back here in 20 minutes appropriately addressed."

"And what would become of the clothes I lent you?"

The Mayor squinted again. "Would you really want them back?"

"Of course I'd want them back. I haven't even had the chance to wear those underpants yet. For your information, wearing silk boxer shorts decorated with pictures of yellow ducks is on my bucket list. That's why I bought them, not to lend them to some unappreciative ponce who'd rather lord it over us by wearing a suit."

"Well!"

"Don't huff at me. You'll have plenty of time to spend your money at the menswear shop once we've done the courteous thing upstairs." Wish-Wash waved his finger at the Mayor. "Don't think I won't want Lambsie back, too — dry-cleaned, thank you very much. And the Hawaiian shirt, I want that back, too." He lowered his voice. "Don't bother washing that again though because I don't want any more pineapples fading away."

———

The meeting went well. Oodles, Wish-Wash and James Northan were given VIP treatment for nearly an hour.

Would they like tea?

Would they like cake?

Sorry they didn't have an elevator. This was directed at Oodles and his walking stick.

Had they had a chance to connect with relatives?

Wish-Wash embraced the tea and cake invitation enthusiastically, but he skirted around any talk of connecting.

The Mayor was more emphatic. He was quite sure he had no relatives left here.

"Are you sure?" the manager said. "What did you say your name was? Northan? I tink you'll find there are a nest of Northans over yer way. Check the local cemetery, too. Dat's always a good starting point for family research."

"Aye," his offsider said. "They couldn't have sent them all to jail."

It was at this point, Wish-Wash ushered the manager away and they disappeared through a door. When they returned from the office, Wish-Wash was holding a small box.

"What have you got there, old son?" Oodles asked.

"I've bought another DNA kit."

"You bought it?" the Mayor smirked. "I thought you said you didn't have any money."

"I'm glad you mentioned that, Jimbo. You don't mind tiding me over?"

"Again? Why do you even need a DNA kit!" The Mayor rolled his eyes. "You don't really think this silly old jumper will reveal any secrets?"

"That's for me to know and for you to find out. Just pay the man, eh?"

———

The Mayor had one hand on the rail as he stamped down the steps and turned his head. "Just how big do you think my credit limit is, Bert? At this rate I won't even be able to afford to buy new clothes."

This wasn't an immediate problem, as it turned out.

When they retraced their steps, they found the menswear shop was already closed.

TWENTY-NINE
'WHAT ARE YOU? CHICKEN?'

"ANYTHING?" Oodles Peered over Wish-Wash's shoulder as he checked his email on the laptop.

They had not long been back from Letterkenny. Even with the dark, it had been a quicker trip home than the one there.

The Mayor had moaned almost non-stop in the car. Wish-Wash had got very excited when he saw a second-hand clothes store on the outskirts of Letterkenny but the Mayor told Oodles to keep driving, for goodness sake, because no way was he desperate enough to lower himself into buying hand-me-downs.

But still he moaned. This fruitless trip to Letterkenny meant another night of him washing the borrowed underpants in the sink, and sentenced him to another day wearing the same stinky pizza shirt, and with this cold he'd have no choice but to wear the jumper for one more day.

He was now taking a shower.

Wish-Wash was lying tummy-down on the bed with the computer lid up.

He turned his head. "Nothing yet. It might have been a mistake to have sent that email to the museum address. Maybe the wrong person opened it? Moose would be the best person to give me some snake-removal tips? It might mean nothing to someone like Katy."

"Perhaps no one's even seen the email because of the time difference." Oodles checked his watch and took a moment to calculate. "It's only early morning there."

"I'm not going back into that kitchen!"

Oodles exhaled. "You're mistaken, old son. James is right for once. It can't possibly be a snake. There are no snakes in Ireland."

"You go down there then!"

"I'm not the one who likes a cup of tea in the middle of the night. If you'd just put on your blinking new glasses, you'd probably see this is all a misunderstanding."

Wish-Wash turned abruptly. "Why would glasses make a difference? The snake is in the cupboard under the sink. No way am I opening it to count its stripes."

"Mice don't have stripes."

"You didn't hear it," Wish-Wash said. "No way was it a mouse. It's a snake, I tell you."

"If you don't open the cupboard to see, you'll never know. What are you? Chicken?" *Beerk, beerk, baaaaarh.*

THIRTY
LETTERKENNY ON THEIR MINDS

"I DON'T WANT to talk about it." The big man rolled over and stared at his empty email in-box. He just stared, as if he were willing Moose to wake up on the other side of the world.

When The Mayor emerged with a towel wrapped around his midriff, he draped the blue boxer shorts with the yellow ducks over the space heater without a word.

He then sat on his bed and started reading the *Reader's Digest* he had found on a bookshelf in the room. A previous guest had left it years ago. It carried an article on the history of typewriters and one about the new president of the United States, Richard Nixon.

Oodles tried to start conversation. "The pub's probably still open if anyone fancies a late snack."

The Mayor grunted. "As if I can go out like this."

"I'm waiting for an email," Wish-Wash said tersely. "Besides, I'm not hungry."

This was new territory for Oodles. He could still remember when the postman used to deliver letters twice a day, now Wish-Wash had discovered email could arrive around the clock he was addicted. It must have been a strong pull to make him go off food.

Oodles sighed. "I'll have the next shower. Is that all right with you blokes?"

Wish-Wash kept his gaze on the screen. "Just don't use up all the hot water."

When Oodles came out of the bathroom in his pyjamas 15 minutes later, Wish-Wash was still staring at the laptop.

"You do know a watched pot never boils, old son. Your turn."

"Fine!" Wish-Wash's venom seemed to be directed more at the computer than anyone. He retrieved his pyjamas from a drawer, picked up the laptop and headed towards the bathroom.

"Where are you going with that?" The Mayor was jerked out of his reading.

Wish-Wash stopped and turned. "You don't think I'd leave it here unguarded, do you?"

"Have you given any thought to what steam does to a computer, Bert."

"It probably gives it a good clean."

The Mayor clenched his eyes shut. "Why don't you leave it with Clarence if you're worried I might try to reclaim it?"

Oodles by now was lying on his bed looking at his e-reader. He looked over the top of his reading glasses, and sighed. "Just put it down on the floor next to me, old son."

Wish-Wash looked at the patch of carpet, then back to the computer. "OK, but don't let *him* get his grubby little hands on it, and if it goes ping come and get me immediately."

———

"Anything?" Wish-Wash said when he emerged from the bathroom dressed for bed in his colourful second-hand pyjamas.

"Nothing," Oodles said.

"Why haven't they answered? It must be 10am back home."

Oodles shrugged. "You never replied to Moose's emails about selling the museum. Perhaps this is payback?"

"But this is clearly serious," Wish-Wash said. "Our lives could be at stake."

Oodles and the Mayor went back to their reading and Wish-Wash went back to staring at the screen. He didn't even notice the Mayor wriggle beneath the blankets, which was a tricky manoeuvre that involved removing his towel but still using it as a modesty shield until it could be safely thrown to the carpet next to his bed. Thing is, he was so anxious that Wish-Wash wouldn't see, he forgot that Oodles had a good view from the other side.

When Elvis ticked over to 10pm a couple of hours later, Oodles removed his glasses. "I'll call it a night. I need some shut-eye." He got up and walked over to the table to put his specs back in their case. Then he went to his suitcase and pulled out his bag of medication, which he brought back to the table so he could sit down and count down what he needed. Blood-pressure tablet, one aspirin, one for cholesterol, one for reflux, and two capsules to keep his arthritis at bay.

Wish-Wash rolled over and watched him. "All those tablets will kill you one day."

"You just worry about yourself, old son. Don't think you can go on looking at that computer all night either. We need to be up bright and early if we want to get to Letterkenny in good time this time." He glanced over to the Mayor. "That OK with you, James?"

"No complaints here." He put the *Reader's Digest* on the floor next to the towel.

Oodles watched him. "Aren't you going to hang that towel up to dry?"

"You're up. Can't you?" the Mayor said.

Wish-Wash seized the chance to add his disgust. "What did your last slave die of, Jimbo?"

"Oh, all right then," the Mayor moaned. "I'll do it as soon as you turn out the lights."

"What? And run the risk you'll trip over something in the dark and break your leg?" Wish-Wash locked eyes with Oodles. "Would they even send an ambulance from Letterkenny at this time of night? That

Conn Northan seems to be a jack-of-all-trades. Perhaps they'd just call him in?"

Oodles did switch off the light at the wall, but only after the Mayor did his nudey run. Oodles and Wish-Wash promised not to look, and they didn't, but the Mayor wasn't to know that.

THIRTY-ONE
TASMANIAN TIGER!

A CRASHING NOISE WOKE OODLES. The luminous clock on the wall said it was 1.15am. Who knew that Elvis glowed in the dark?

When Oodles lifted his head and saw a large shape groping around on the table, he figured something had been knocked over.

"What are you looking for, old son?" Oodles whispered.

"I'm just getting my glasses," Wish-Wash replied. "I haven't slept a wink yet. I'm going downstairs to make a cuppa."

"Your glasses? About time! Changed your mind about going to the kitchen, too, eh?"

"That's why I've decided to wear the goggles. It's the only way you and the Mayor are going to believe a poisonous snake is hiding in the kitchen."

"You're going to open the cupboard?"

"You're half the reason I've been lying awake thinking. I'm no chicken!"

"What will you do if you open it and there really is a snake looking at you?"

"I don't know. Does the *Guinness Book of Records* have a category for speed of closing cupboards?"

———

James Northan slept through this exchange.

But he awoke a few minutes later when Wish-Wash burst back into the room and flicked on the light.

"It's worse than I thought," Wish-Wash wheezed, having run up the stairs two steps at a time. "Forget what I said about the snake. It's actually a Tasmanian Tiger under the sink."

"Oh, for goodness sake!" The Mayor sat up and rubbed his eyes. He did a double-take when he saw Wish-Wash was finally wearing his spectacles.

"I think you'd better sit down, old son." Oodles said as he threw back the blankets and stepped on to the cold carpet.

Wish-Wash sat down at the table and put his head into his arms. "My heart is racing. I think I need one of your blood-pressure tablets, Oodles."

Oodles sat down next to him and put a hand on the back of Wish-Wash's Cherokee Indian-pattern pyjamas. "Breathe in, breathe out. You'll be fine. Tell us what happened, big fella?"

"Oh, for goodness sake! Don't humour him," the Mayor said from his bed.

Wish-Wash glanced up, with fogged-up glasses. "Why is it you never believe me?"

The Mayor yawned. "I don't know. Could it be because you've been making up stories since 1967?"

Wish-Wash banged a fist on the table. "Why would I make this up?" he said, his voice rising. "You rotten mongrel bastard!"

Oodles reached over and massaged Wish-Wash's neck. "You've got to calm down. Keep breathing in and out."

Wish-Wash removed his glasses and put them on the table, which had now stopped vibrating. He looked sideways. "You believe me, don't you cobber?"

"Why wouldn't I believe you?" Oodles said. "People have been claiming to see Tasmanian Tigers for years."

"Oh, for goodness sake," the Mayor said again. "Sensible people don't even believe those claims in Tasmania. You really think a sighting in Ireland is more credible? Please!"

"It's possible," Oodles said. "The Tasmanian Tiger used to live in other parts of Australia, so why not in Ireland, too? Maybe it got trapped here when the seas rose?"

"Oh, for goodness sake! I expected better of you, Clarence."

" I just don't think you can rule it in or out. It wasn't that many years ago a majority of people thought the world was flat." He glared at the Mayor. "Some people still do!"

"And you think it might have been trapped by rising seas in the cupboard downstairs!" the Mayor said. "Spare me!"

"It's not trapped in the cupboard any more."

Oodles and the Mayor both looked at Wish-Wash.

"That's what I was trying to tell you. When I plucked up the courage to open the cupboard, I expected to see the beady little eyes of a snake looking back at me, so it was a shock to see a Tasmanian Tiger snarling."

"You didn't close the cupboard, old son?"

Wish-Wash looked back at Oodles. "Are you kidding? I don't know how I even had the presence of mind to drop my teabag. I hightailed it out of the kitchen as fast as I could."

"But you managed to close the kitchen door behind you?" Oodles asked.

"Yes. By the time I heard it slam, I was already at the bottom of the stairs."

"So it might have got out?"

"I heard it yelp, so I don't think so." Wish-Wash buried his head in his hands again. "I've had a near-death experience."

"Oh for goodness sake," the Mayor said. "Since when did Tasmanian Tigers eat people? You'd have more chance of being consumed by a hungry leprechaun in this part of the world."

Wish-Wash lifted his head. "As if I'm going to believe a word you say! I'm telling you what I saw. With my own eyes!"

Wish-Wash insisted he had to send an email to the gang in Windy Mountain right away. He said he had worked out why Moose hadn't replied about the snake. Reptiles weren't his area of expertise. He was probably consulting a real expert, and that stuff took time. But he'd want to know about this turn of events. Tasmanian Tigers were in his wheelhouse. It wouldn't surprise Wish-Wash if he was on the next plane.

"Oh, for goodness sake," the Mayor said. "Do I have to remind you gentlemen we need to be up early to go to Letterkenny?"

"This is important." Wish-Wash flopped on to his bed, opened the laptop and adjusted his glasses as if they weren't quite sitting right. "Sooner I send it, sooner we get some expert advice."

"From Moose?" The Mayor looked towards the roof. "That man is an imbecile."

Wish-Wash thumped the mattress. "He's devoted most of his blinking adult life to finding the Tasmanian Tiger."

"I rest my case. Only a moron would flog that dead horse."

Wish-Wash pressed on the trackpad. "I'll be quick."

"You jest!" the Mayor said. "You said the email you composed last night wouldn't take long. But we had to lie awake for more than an hour listening to your one-finger typing."

"I'll be faster now I'm starting to work out where the keys are. I don't know who decided the keys shouldn't be an alphabetical order."

The Mayor rolled his eyes. "That might have been Christopher Latham Sholes who invented the QUERTY keyboard in 1868." He was such a know-all!

"Christopher who?" Wish-Wash lifted his head and stared at the wall. "Are you sure it wasn't Steve Jobs?"

The Mayor sunk beneath the doona, groaning.

Oodles knew he did have a point.

Wish-Wash hadn't got the hang of writing snappy emails. Oodles had seen his handiwork. Often written with the CAPSLOCK on, they were always long and convoluted. Oodles had no doubt this email would be even longer.

They really did need to get to Letterkenny in the morning, too.

As much as he enjoyed seeing James bring out his wallet every time they had a bill to pay, the joke was wearing thin.

And as much as he enjoyed seeing the Mayor in humiliating clothes, enough is sometimes enough.

But what was the point of trying to sleep?

If Wish-Wash was intent on sending the email, another prima donna pulling the covers over his head wasn't going to stop him.

Oodles figured he might as well pick up where he left off on that novel he was reading.

He collected his e-reader from his bedside table and returned to the table.

He opened up his glasses case, but it was empty.

It was then he realised what had happened.

He looked over at Wish-Wash lying face-down on his bed compiling his email. He was wearing Oodles's glasses and he didn't even know it.

Of course! They had both purchased identical frames. Goody had apologised they were so dusty. But he had said they were last year's frames, which made them cheaper. They both came in free red cases — identical cases embossed in the same gold lettering: *Walter Moncrieff. Fine Eyewear. Slutz Plains.*

Wish-Wash wouldn't have known the difference.putting them on in the dark.

Oodles glanced over at Wish-Wash again. He appeared to be coping with the wrong prescription. How effective reading glasses would have been identifying a Tasmanian Tiger hiding in a kitchen cupboard was more doubtful.

———

Wish-Wash closed the computer lid just after 2am, and returned the glasses to the case on the table.

His hand now hovered over the light switch next to the door. "Ready?"

Oodles closed his book and put his e-reader on his bedside table. He hadn't said anything to Wish-Wash about him wearing the wrong glasses. He had merely bumped up the type size on his e-reader.

No reply came at all from the bundle under the Mayor's covers. Either he wasn't talking or he really had fallen asleep.

"What did you say about the snake, old son?" Oodles said.

"I was in two minds," Wish-Wash said. "Since no one replied, perhaps they didn't even get that email. I might have sent it to the wrong address, I guess. But the more I thought about it, I decided it'd be rude of me not to even mention it. I mean, what if they are just waiting on advice from a snake catcher? They'd think I'd just been having a lend of them."

"So, what did you tell them?"

"I said it was a misunderstanding." He smiled mischievously. "I said that was all Jimbo's fault."

The bundle was suddenly unbundled as the covers were cast aside. "You said what?"

"You are awake then, Jimbo?" Wish-Wash switched off the light. "Love to chat, but it really is sleep-time."

————

Oodles didn't know how Wish-Wash did it.

He switched on the light again at 6.30am.

Oodles blinked against the flood of light. His body clock said he ought to be thinking of going back to sleep.

"Come on you sloths." Wish-Wash had already dressed. He was back in his emerald green suit. But that canary yellow shirt was a new one on Oodles.

The Mayor lifted his head and gave him a look like a cat's arse. "How can you be so cheerful at this time of the morning?"

Wish-Wash walked over and opened the curtains, which did nothing at all to further lighten the room but intensified the sound of the rain out there in the dark.

"I can almost smell the bacon cooking," he said.

"You can have *all* my breakfast this time." The Mayor plunged his head back face down in his pillow.

Wish-Wash walked over and prodded him. "You're the one keen to get to Letterkenny!"

The Mayor lifted his head again. "Yes, but if I skip breakfast I can sleep in for another half an hour."

Wish-Wash sighed. "Please yourself. But don't blame me if—"

The Mayor had fallen back into sleep.

Wish-Wash went to shake him again but Oodles said, "Leave him. We'll collect him on the way out."

Wish-Wash turned and watched Oodles head towards the bathroom.

"Don't you want to hear what Moose said?" Wish-Wash said.

Oodles stopped and turned. "They've replied?" he gasped.

"The email arrived about an hour ago."

"What's it say?"

Wish-Wash pumped out his chest. "Moose says if we've really caught a Tasmanian Tiger in Ireland it's going to be worth a million dollars."

Oodles muttered under his breath. "Or a free set of new glasses."

Wish-Wash curled his lip. "What did you say, cobber?"

Oodles ran a hand over his hair. "I said, um, if that happens, we'll have to raise our glasses."

"We have to catch it first. Good news is Moose has explained what we have to do." He looked at the breathing shape he knew was the Mayor. "You sure I can't wake him? I want to see the look on his face when he hears Moose has already come up with a plan. He's going to regret calling a genius an imbecile."

"He didn't say anything more about the sale of the museum?"

"Nope."

"And you haven't heard back from Rod?"

"No, I haven't heard from the rotten little waster."

"Hmm, so what is this brilliant plan of Moose's?"

"I'll tell you over breakfast. I'll bring the laptop with us in case Jimbo wakes up and gets any funny ideas."

THIRTY-TWO
JAR OF HONEY AND A BALL
OF STRING

THEY WERE a third the way to Letterkenny when Oodles pulled over.

"Why have you stopped the car?" Wish-Wash said.

Oodles slumped over the steering wheel and pinched the bridge of his nose. "Tiredness has come over me like a wave. One of you two blokes will have to drive."

"Christ Almighty!" Wish-Wash said. "We've been through this before. I haven't even got a licence and it's even worse now. The cops are sure to notice me in broad daylight."

Oodles and Wish-Wash turned their heads towards the back at the same time.

"Looks like it's over to you—" Oodles started to say before he realised the Mayor wasn't even there.

He slapped his forehead. "Oh no, we've forgotten him. All that talk over brekky about Moose's plan distracted us big time. We'll have to turn back and get him." He turned the ignition back on.

Wish-Wash reached over and held the steering wheel. "I thought you were too jet-lagged to drive?"

Oodles gave him a pained look. "I think the surge of adrenalin has woken me up. James will be livid."

"It's his own silly fault," Wish-Wash said. "He's the one who wanted to sleep in. I did try to warn him."

"You planned this?"

"How could I plan it? It's just a lucky break."

"Don't you think it's time to ease up on him."

Wish-Wash pulled at his beard. "No flaming way! Do you realise how many years he's been lording it over us?"

"I can't believe you made him waste his money on the DNA kit so you can trace Lambsie's heritage to Peru. What if he's right? What if it really comes from the Tasmanian midlands?"

Wish-Wash started laughing. "Lambsie coming from Peru is just a line I fed him to get a reaction. Mission accomplished! Truth is the jumper is probably not even made out of real wool. It used to have a made-in-China tag on it."

Oodles squinted at him. "So what's the DNA kit you put under your bed for?"

"Ah, I'm going to try to prove the Mayor and Conn Northan are related."

"You are?" Oodles threw his head back into the head-rest and laughed. "Good luck getting a DNA sample from James! You think he's going to happily give you a mouth swab?"

Wish-Wash stroked the double-chin that was hidden under his beard. "I've been giving that some thought. I've got a Plan A and a Plan B."

"Which are?"

"He's bound to leave some strands of hair on Lambsie."

"It could be anybody's hair!"

"I really didn't want to fall back on Plan B."

"Which is?"

"The underpants I lent him."

"Oh, that's gross." Oodles screwed up his face. "But the problem is much the same. You don't know how many people have worn those undies."

"Hmm, you're right." Wish-Wash rubbed the back of his neck. "I'll have to give this some more thought."

He barely said anything for the rest of the road trip.

They changed their money in Letterkenny, and it was a novelty not having to ask James Northan to pay for the jar of honey or the ball of string.

On their return trip, they even went to that second-hand store Wish-Wash had seen on the outskirts of Letterkenny, and emerged from the shop each with peaked hats.

They stopped halfway for lunch in a village pub.

———

The Mayor was livid when they walked into the B&B bedroom. "You forgot me deliberately, didn't you?"

There was something different about him.

Oodles took a moment to work out what it was, then it hit him.

Lambsie was no where in sight. The Mayor was wearing jeans, wellington boots, a tweed peak cap just like the ones they were wearing and a blue-grey sweater that wouldn't have looked out of place on a fisherman.

"What's with the change of clobber, old son?" Oodles said.

The Mayor continued to stare coldly. "I had to take things into my own hands, didn't I?"

"But we drove around looking. There are no clothing stores in this village."

"No, but a woman named Maggie sells second-hand clothes from her caravan, which she parks up near the castle. When I woke up around 10am and realised you two had deserted me, Cathleen pointed me in that direction."

Wish-Wash gave a single clap like a pair of cymbals providing the exclamation mark for an orchestra. *Hee-haw, hee-haw.* "Second hand? I thought you swore you'd never lower yourself that far again?"

The Mayor looked like he had an unpleasant taste in his mouth. "That's before I realised I couldn't rely on you two to get me to

Letterkenny. Anyway, Maggie assured me not all this lot is second-hand. The tweed jacket in the wardrobe is and so is this hat."

He brushed his hand down the right side of the sweater. "This lot is brand new though, so are the boxers and socks I bought."

"You've fitted yourself out properly then?" Oodles said.

"I had to. I couldn't bear to wear that woolly monstrosity one more day!"

"That's charming, that is," Wish-Wash said. "I'm getting no thanks for saving you from freezing to death? I presume you found a back-yard dry-cleaners, too."

The Mayor looked from face to face. "I thought you were only joking when you said you wanted that old jumper back, Bert?"

"Why would I joke about it?"

"And you really wanted that faded shirt back?"

"And those underpants!" Wish-Wash continued without stopping to take a breath, which made his face go progressively red. "And those nice pink socks! I want those back, too. Flaming heck I do. And don't dare forget the Sydney Swans beanie! I might have to support them again if the Hawks have a bad season."

"Really?"

"Yes, really." Wish-Wash put the jar of honey and ball of string down on the table and sucked in some air. "Didn't I tell you those underpants were on my bucket list!"

"I thought you were joking."

"What have you done with them?"

"Ah." The Mayor's face creased into frown lines. "Maggie has a trade-in scheme."

Wish-Wash shook a trembling finger at him. "You mean to tell me you swapped *my* clothes for those clothes?"

"Not exactly, no. I bought rather more than I left there. I had to pay for the balance."

"But you don't have any cash, Jimbo," Wish-Wash raged.

"I was surprised Maggie took a credit card, too, tell you the truth.

Funniest-looking EFTPOS machine I've ever seen but it seemed to make all the right noises when I keyed in my password."

"We'll have to go get my stuff back," Wish-Wash huffed. "If you have to pay some extra, tough! Just as soon as I soak this string in honey, we're returning to the castle."

The Mayor looked from face to face again. He spoke slowly. "Soak the string in honey? Why would you want to do that?"

"It's what Moose said to do," Wish-Wash said. "He says it's the best way to catch our Tasmanian Tiger."

"Oh my Lord! He said that! And you believed him? The man really is an imbecile!"

Wish-Wash glared. "Who are you to call anyone an imbecile? You're as dumb as a bag of hammers."

THIRTY-THREE
NOW YOU SEE IT, NOW YOU DON'T

THE MAYOR POINTED to the wheel ruts. "See, I didn't make this up. The caravan *was* here."

"Well, it's not here now." Wish-Wash glowered. "Nor is Lambsie."

"Sorry, Bert, I really am." The Mayor had perfected the politician's way of sounding contrite even if he wasn't. "I'll buy you another jumper. Goodness, I'll buy you a whole flock of Lambsies if it makes you feel better."

Wish-Wash continued to scowl. "You'd probably have to go all the way to Peru to do that, and I'd wager you'd need to go to Hawaii to get another shirt like that. And don't get me started about those underpants! I can't even think how far afield you'd need to go to get them. Russia probably."

The Mayor looked at Oodles and rolled his eyes. "Isn't global trade a wonderful thing that all these items ended up on a shelf together at the Slutz Plains op shop?"

"Are you taking the piss?" Wish-Wash said.

"What do you expect me to do? Wave my magic wand and make them all come back? Oh, I haven't actually got a magic wand! Oodles, can I borrow your walking stick? For goodness sake, Bert, you can see from the blasted tracks I'm not lying about the caravan being here this morning."

"You'd better find out where it's gone."

The Mayor sighed. "Lucky for you, that shouldn't be a problem. Cathleen says she knows everyone who lives in this village, right?"

"You better hope she does." Wish-Wash had flecks of white froth on his upper lip. "Until I get back those blue boxers with the yellow ducks, every man I meet in this village will wonder why I can't look them in the eye. I'll be too fixated on what they might be wearing below."

"Oh, for heaven's sake, Bert! Can you at least have the decency to wait till Clarence and I aren't in the room with you before you start staring at their crotches!"

"If someone accuses me of being a pervert, I'll tell them straight out who put me up to it." He pointed an accusing finger.

———

Cathleen stopped her polishing and looked up when the old men came into reception. "You still haven't laid eyes on Donal and Mary?"

Oodles shook his head. "Nope."

Cathleen waved the cloth she had been using to buff the table. "I'll tan their hides if I catch them with dat dog. I know they are hiding him."

Of course! Oodles suddenly knew exactly where the dog was secreted. He wanted to tell her to try the guest kitchen. Judging by the looks on their faces, Wish-Wash and James hadn't made the same connection.

They both obviously had Lambsie on their mind.

The Mayor cleared his throat. "Thanks, by the way, for giving me the heads up on that clothing van, Cathleen."

"All grand? How did it go?"

"I got a range of new clothes." He patted his sweater. "As you can see."

"Oh aye. Is Maggie selling new stuff now?" Cathleen gave the slightest hint of a snigger.

Wish-Wash gave the Mayor's shoulder a not-so-gentle push. "Go on," he mouthed.

The Mayor cleared his throat again. "Thing is, we've just all been back there — and the caravan has gone."

Cathleen glanced up at the clock on the wall. "Aye, I expect it has. She only parks there of a morning."

"Oh good. So if we go back first thing in the morning and wait for her—."

Her giggling stopped him. "You'll be waiting quite a while, you will," Cathleen said. "She won't be back until dis time next month."

"Next month!" Wish-Wash cried.

"But only in the morning. She moves the caravan to another village after lunch."

The blood drained from Wish-Wash's face. "I doubt we'll still even be here in a month."

"Will you not?" Redness rose to her cheeks. "That Malachy! Telling Shamus more fibs again! The way I heard it you'd be here until the castle renovation is finished!"

"He said that?" Wish-Wash looked around at the other old men. "Can you direct us to Maggie's home? We can go there."

"I'm not sure she takes returns," Cathleen said.

"This isn't about taking anything back," Wish-Wash said. "It's about getting things back that still belong to me." His tone conveyed urgency. "So can you help us?"

"Naw, not really. I don't have her address."

The Mayor's eyes widened. "I thought you knew everyone in this village!"

"Oh, I do. I know where they all live, too, even the ones now in the graveyard, God rest their souls."

"But not Maggie?"

"Naw. She doesn't actually live in dis village."

The Mayor raked his hair. "You're kidding me! Where does she live?"

Cathleen shrugged. "I don't know."

The Mayor's voice rose. "You don't know? Someone must know. This is important!"

Cathleen placed the tin of furniture polish against her left cheek. "Hmm. I could ask Shamus to check with her son. He might know."

"Her son?"

"Yes, her son *does* live in dis village. You must have met him at the pub?"

THIRTY-FOUR
A 2000-YEAR TRADITION

WISH-WASH AND OODLES followed the Mayor when he stormed out of the room. Wish-Wash latched on to his shoulder at the bottom of the stairs and turned him around. "What do you think you're playing at, Jimbo?"

"I am not dealing with Conn Northan. Besides, he probably doesn't even know where his mother lives. If she's got any sense, she has moved home and not given him a forwarding address."

"Where's that leave me?"

The Mayor exhaled noisily. "I told you. I'll buy you a whole new outfit. Get Oodles to drive us back to Letterkenny and I'll get you whatever you like."

Wish-Wash's scowl changed to a smile "Anything I want?"

"Within reason?"

"New stuff?"

"Those clothes were second-hand!"

Wish-Wash eyeballed him. "They were barely used!"

"Don't try to extort me, Bert. I'm trying to be fair and reasonable here."

"We can always go over to the pub right now. Conn Northan is bound to be there."

The Mayor looked down at his shoes, then up again. "Fine! I said I'd buy you anything you'd like, didn't I?"

Wish-Wash spat on his hand and offered it. "Swear!"

The Mayor looked down at the hand and wrinkled his nose. "Who taught you that disgusting habit?"

"If you must know, Moose did."

"Him? I didn't think he had any room to slip further in my estimation."

"Are you going to swear, or not?"

"Not this way, for goodness sake! You'll need to go wash your hand before I shake it."

Oodles nodded at Wish-Wash. "Let it go, old son. I'm a witness." He sighed noisily. "We'll go back to Letterkenny tomorrow."

———

Oodles watched Wish-Wash feed the honey-soaked string under the kitchen door.

He didn't have the heart to tell him the animal he had seen had most likely been the fugitive dog Donal and Mary had hidden away. It figured. If the old men hadn't seen the kids, the kids had probably no idea of their existence either. They might have assumed the B&B was customer-less, which meant the kitchen would have been a perfectly good sanctuary — and the cupboard under the sink provided an extra layer of secrecy.

The surprising thing to Oodles was that the Mayor hadn't figured it out, too. Then again, he hadn't been privy to Wish-Wash picking up the wrong glasses. It's a wonder the big man hadn't tripped down the stairs with that distorted vision!

The Mayor just blamed Wish-Wash's latest sighting on a wild imagination rather than mistaken identity.

For his part, Wish-Wash seemed happier with the state of affairs now he knew he was going to be treated to a new wardrobe of clothes in Letterkenny.

He had splashed some water on his face up in the en suite then announced there was work to be done back downstairs. He made the Mayor carry down the honey jar and the string because he said that was his job.

"Either Moose is even more stupid than I thought or he's having a lend of you," The Mayor ranted as Wish-Wash got on to his knees and started threading the string under the door. "I'm surprised they even have honey here in Ireland."

Wish-Wash turned around and looked up at him. "Ah, that's where you're wrong. Oodles and I looked it up on the computer, didn't we cobber? They've been making honey in Ireland for 2000 years."

The Mayor tutted. "And how many Tasmanian Tigers have they caught with it in that period of time?"

"You can laugh. But Moose knows his stuff." Wish-Wash pointed to the label on the jar of honey, which was sitting next to him on the wooden floor. "Made by bees in south-eastern Ireland, see?"

"Very good," the Mayor said. "But I can't even hear a noise on the other side of that door."

"Have you turned your hearing aids on?"

The Mayor raised fingers to the on-switches. "Yes. Happy?"

"It still doesn't mean you're not a deaf bugger. And probably a dumb one, too. If Moose says it will work, it will bloody-well work."

THIRTY-FIVE
'I KNOW WHAT I SAW'

WHEN THE OLD men went down to breakfast, Wish-Wash insisted on making a detour to the guest kitchen.

A length of the honey-soaked string was still sticking out from beneath the door, just as they had left it.

"I don't understand it?" Wish-Wash bent down on one knee to inspect the string. "Moose said this would work."

"What did I tell you?" The Mayor flashed a supercilious smile. "The man's a moron!"

Wish-Wash turned his head. "Perhaps I didn't do all the steps right?"

"Oh, for goodness sake, Bert, he only gave you four steps!" The Mayor counted them on his hand. "Buy string. Buy honey. Soak string in honey. Thread under door." He frowned. "It didn't even involve hooks. How in the Lord's name was it supposed to work?"

"Moose wouldn't use hooks! Ever heard of sedation?"

"With honey?"

"It might have that effect on Tasmanian Tigers?" Wish-Wash pulled the Mayor down to floor level. "See what you can hear?"

The Mayor put his left ear to the door and listened.

After almost a minute, he pulled back. "I can't hear a thing."

Wish-Wash smiled. "What did I tell you? Sedation. The Tasmanian Tiger's probably sound asleep."

Oodles pinched the bridge of his nose. "How do you explain, old son, that the string appears untouched at this end?"

Wish-Wash shrugged. "Maybe this Tasmanian Tiger is a dainty eater?"

By now, the Mayor had returned to his feet. "Another theory is there's nothing really in there."

"I know what I saw," Wish-Wash said.

Oodles rolled his eyes. This didn't seem to be the right moment to tell Wish-Wash about the mix-up with the glasses. He didn't want to humiliate him in front of the Mayor.

Wish-Wash used the doorknob to hoist himself up. "If you're so sure there's nothing in there, Jimbo, why don't you step inside and see."

"Me?" The Mayor's voice rose to a shriek.

"You did agree to carry the bags."

"I didn't agree to this."

He was saved by the growl coming from the other side of the door.

"Oh, great!" Wish-Wash said. "See what you've done now? You've only woken it up with your shouting!"

———

Cathleen looked surprised when she came into the breakfast room and found Wish-Wash and Oodles sitting at one table, and James Northan sitting behind them on his own.

"What can I get you?" she asked Wish-Wash and Oodles.

"Two full Irish breakfasts and two cups of tea, love," Wish-Wash said.

She turned around to the Mayor. "And you?"

"He wants toast with honey," Wish-Wash shouted.

"Don't listen to him, Cathleen," the Mayor said, his voice straining to remain calm. "But I don't want an Irish breakfast like that pig. I'll just use the breakfast bar, if that's OK."

Oodles saw him go up four times to help himself to cereal and fruit. He ate like a man who hadn't eaten for a couple of days — which, when Oodles thought of it, he probably hadn't.

Speaking with his mouth full of egg, bacon and black pudding had never been a problem for Wish-Wash, but this time the only noise was the sound of him munching.

"Are you all right, old son?" Oodles said.

Wish-Wash swallowed. "I'm trying to work out what to tell Moose?"

"If I were you, I'd leave it until we come back from Letterkenny. It'd be night at home now. Let him read it with a fresh mind."

Wish-Wash sprayed Oodles with bacon fat as he waved his fork. "How could Jimbo say he couldn't hear it growling? You believe me now, don't you cobber?"

Oodles dabbed at his face with his serviette, and sighed. "Let's see what Moose says."

THIRTY-SIX
'I CAN TIE A REEF KNOT.
THAT ANY GOOD?'

THE ROAD TRIP to Letterkenny started like this:

"Oodles, will you remind Jimbo he said he'd get whatever I wanted in Letterkenny."

"Clarence, will you explain to Bert what *within reason* means."

"Oodles, will you tell the Mayor what his *obligations* are."

"Clarence, will you remind Bert he only lent me one set of clothes, and what *quid pro quo* means."

"Enough!" Oodles finally cried. "You want me to stop the car so you can both walk to Letterkenny!"

They continued the rest of the trip in silence.

———

Finding a parking spot was easier than two days before. The sky was sullen but the rain was holding off.

They sat in the car casing the street.

Wish-Wash finally pointed. "There! That's where I want to go."
Oodles and the Mayor followed his finger direction.

"Oh for goodness sake," the Mayor said. "That's the shop I wanted to go to — only it was closed."

"I can see it's open now," Wish-Wash said. "Look, there's someone dressing that dummy in the window."

"Really, Bert? I think you'll find they are called mannequins in proper tailor shops."

"Oh, la ti da." Wish-Wash turned his head towards the back seat. "You don't think I've ever been to a *proper tailor shop*, do you?"

"I didn't say that," the Mayor said. "But wouldn't you be happier if we can find you a nice shop that does second-hand clothes. Be with your own people?"

"My own people? What people would they be?"

"You said it. Dummies."

Wish-Wash shook a fist at the Mayor. "Who made you God's gift to men's fashion? I don't need Oodles to explain *quid pro quo* to me. I get that you will only buy me one set of clothes — but that …" he pointed again. "… is where I want to go shopping."

————

"This is ridiculous, Bert," the Mayor said, as the salesman pinned Wish-Wash's trouser bottoms. "You've never worn a three-piece pinstripe suit in your life."

"How would you know?" Wish-Wash looked straight ahead into the full-length mirror.

The Mayor held the steely gaze that reflected back to him. "I think I'd know if the Slutz Plains op shop had branched out into super-fine merino wool suits. You do know the wool for this suit might have been sourced in Tasmania?"

The tailor looked up. "Dis is made in Italy, sir."

"That's fair then — quid pro quo for Lambsie." Wish-Wash stood ramrod straight, not even moving a facial muscle. "I was wrong about Peru, as it happens. But it turns out Lambsie was actually made in

China out of Australian wool, so there is still an international connection."

"Oh, for goodness sake!" The Mayor glared at Wish-Wash's reflection. "You're not seriously trying to compare the greasy wool that came from a two-tooth mutton to the super-fine fleece of a merino sheep?"

Wish-Wash squinted. "Are you denigrating sheep now?"

The Mayor sighed and addressed the tailor, who was on his knees. "When will the alterations be ready?"

The tailor took the last pin out of his mouth. "Nearly done here. If sirs would like to come back in an hour."

Wish-Wash turned his head to protest. "I haven't picked out my flaming shirt and tie yet!"

"Oh, Lordy!" The Mayor pinched his eyebrows. "Do you even know how to tie a Windsor knot?"

"We're not going anywhere near Buckingham Palace."

The Mayor closed his eyes. "It's the knot that one uses to tie one's ties."

"Oh, does *one*. I can tie a reef knot. That any good?"

"Oh, for goodness sake!"

Wish-Wash spent some time choosing the checked shirt and the striped purple and pink tie, which he said he was sure would go well with his new green pinstripe suit.

The look on the Mayor's face told Oodles not everyone agreed.

The tailor tucked the shirt and tie under the counter. "Would sir like to pay now? Oh excellent," he said when James Northan handed him his credit card.

Then the tailor handed him the bill, and punched in some numbers into the portable EFTPOS machine.

The Mayor studied the bill and gasped.

"Everything in order, sir?" The tailor handed him the machine. "Just tap in yer pin number, if you please."

The Mayor obliged and the machine whirred.

The tailor looked down at it, and then up at the Mayor. "Oh dear, yer card has been declined, sir."

THIRTY-SEVEN
MAGGIE NORTHAN'S DAMN CARAVAN

As THEY WALKED AWAY from the tailor shop, the Mayor's phone beeped.

He told the two other men to wait while he checked the incoming text message. It wasn't easy to stop because people were coming both ways.

But the Mayor was oblivious as he groaned while looking down at his phone.

"What's the matter, old son?" Oodles said.

"It's from my bank," the Mayor said. "They've cancelled my credit card because it was used to buy $10,000 worth of jewellery in Milan last night, which they thought was suspicious because they know I'm in Ireland."

"How do they know that?" Wish-Wash looked skyward. He was probably scouring the air for satellites, drones or spy pigeons. All he would have seen though were black clouds.

"Oh, for goodness sake!" the Mayor said. "Didn't you inform your bank where you'd be when?"

"It's none of their business where I am," Wish-Wash said brusquely.

Oodles felt the need to elaborate. "Katy did register us with Smart

Traveller so the government knows where we are if there is a potato famine or something."

Wish-Wash scratched his head. "Yeah, I had forgotten about that. They wanted to know where we'll be when and who we're with."

The Mayor squinted at him. "Who you're with?"

"Yeah, they wanted to know if we were travelling with any drongos, so we provided your name."

The Mayor realised he had just taken the bait. "Oh, that's a nice thing to say at a time like this. You do realise I now have no means of paying for anything. I'm destitute."

Wish-Wash pointed to a nearby park bench just beyond the shelter of the awning. "That looks freshly painted to me. There was a time I'd regard that as luxury accommodation!"

"That's the level of compassion I'd expect from you."

"Like I've had any sort of an apology from you!" Wish-Wash held up his thumb and index finger. "I came this close to getting my first new pinstripe suit."

"Ah ha," the Mayor said. "You're admitting it now, are you? You've never even had a pinstripe suit!"

"I said *new*, you deaf old git. But you're right on this being the first time for me. I've never been kicked out of a clothing shop before. And it's your bloody fault."

"My fault? That card could have been skimmed anywhere. McDonald's? That'd rate as *your* fault! The pub? A service station? The B&B? Definitely all your fault, every one of them. Or ..." He buried his head in his hands as realisation set in. "Maggie Northan's damn caravan," he said in a faltering voice.

———

The Mayor's text gave him a 24-hour-number to ring. He had global roaming, so he did it straight away.

Most people put the phone to their ear.

But James Northan was in the habit of putting it on speaker phone and holding the handset at arm's length to minimise his risk of getting brain cancer.

The downside was everyone else in the vicinity could hear, too.

This normally didn't worry him.

But today it did.

He was one digit out. He called a 24-hour Sydney sex line by mistake. The woman who answered it seemed to be having an orgasm, which turned a lot of heads in the Letterkenny city centre.

"Oh, for goodness sake, woman." The Mayor hung up and checked the number again.

This time he got it right.

Someone answered straight away and knew exactly what he was talking about.

So just as they thought? He really wasn't the jewellery buyer in Milan? It happened quite a bit actually. Where had he used the card? He hadn't used it in Dubai? Oh, someone must had got hold of his details in Ireland and relayed them.

Yes, they could issue him with a new card.

Was there somewhere they could mail it?

The Mayor clicked his fingers. "Quick, Clarence, give me the address of the B&B?"

Oodles shrugged and looked up at Wish-Wash, who was twiddling his bound-up umbrella. "Don't look at me. I'd have to go back to the car and look it up in the guidebook." His eyes lit up. "I know the castle address, if that's any help."

"Oh, spare me." The Mayor waved the phone.

He spoke into it again. Would it be possible, he asked, for the new card to be sent to a bank in Dublin and be held for him to pick up? He'd be in Dublin in 10 days' time. Just let him know which bank it was going to.

THIRTY-EIGHT
ADD SOME SHOES TO THE SHOPPING LIST

WISH-WASH BROKE the silence on the drive home. "Do you think I should send that email when we get back, Oodles?"

"Please yourself, old mate, but it's late in the night back in Windy Mountain, which means no one is going to be awake to read it," Oodles said as the windscreen wipers swished. "Best to wait a bit longer. I was thinking we'd be back early enough for a spot of lunch at the pub."

The Mayor groaned. "Oh, do we have to?"

"We have to eat, James." Oodles caught him in the rear-view mirror. He looked very, very unhappy.

"You know I haven't got any money now!"

"You know we'll lend you some money." Oodles glanced sideways towards Wish-Wash. "Won't we?"

"I won't," the big man said. "Not until he meets his obligations."

"One's thing for certain." Oodles said. "You'll have to wait now until we go to Dublin to hit the menswear shops."

Wish-Wash blew out his cheeks. "I reckon he can throw in a new pair of shoes. Accrued interest."

―――――

Malachy Willson was the first to see them come through the door.

"Speak of the devils? Look who's here!" Then he realised Wish-Wash wasn't with them. "Where's my cousin?"

"He'll be along soon," Oodles said. "He's just gone back to our room to send an email. I told him no one would be awake to read it, but he's a bit pig-headed." He sat down on a stool. "Are we too late for a spot of lunch?"

"Course not." Malachy sucked on a cigarette and blew out a stream of blue smoke. "The lamb is on special today."

"For goodness sake!" The Mayor fanned the air with his hands. "I thought smoking was banned in Irish drinking establishments."

Malachy took joy in taking another long puff and this time aimed the stream of smoke towards the Mayor. "Who's going to tell on me?"

This was the moment the man sitting two stools up from Oodles turned around. They hadn't recognised him from behind because he wasn't wearing his suit today. But as their eyes met, the Mayor knew exactly who he was.

"I didn't think you were ever going to talk to me?" Conn Northan said.

James Northan looked back, gape-mouthed.

"Ma didn't waste any time moving my old clothes on then?" Conn said.

The Mayor looked down at his tightly-knitted sweater. "Your clothes? What do you mean?"

Conn looked around at the landlord. "Tell him, Malachy."

Malachy nodded. "Seems strange someone else walking in wearing yer old clothes, Conn."

Conn dismounted his stool, walked over and grabbed one of the Mayor's sleeves. "Got to give Ma credit. She cleaned this well. You can't see where the fish guts were now."

The Mayor looked towards the roof. "Lord, please tell me it's not true!"

"Oh, it's true all right," Conn said. "Sweater, jeans, wellies. I swapped them for a share of one of the nice suits she had in."

"A share?"

"Aye, I wear it for two days and Paddy O'Hare wears it for the next two days." He pointed to a drinker on the other end of the bar who indeed was wearing the grey pinstripe suit.

"Oh, for goodness sake!" The Mayor's eyes looked up again. "This is getting worse."

"I tink you are exaggerating," Conn said. "I trust Ma gave you a good deal?" He started laughing. It was a deep rumbling belly-laugh that ended with him bending over and clasping his knees. "She didn't claim those clothes were new, did she?"

The Mayor stood to his full height. "No, but she didn't tell me who used to own them. I'm only glad the underpants and socks *were* new."

"Dat so?" Conn wiped tears from his eyes with his knuckles. "The underpants aren't red, by any chance?"

———

The Mayor was still recovering his equilibrium when Wish-Wash came through the door.

The big man had changed. He was back in his green and swirly orange tracksuit pants.

Oodles and the Mayor had fled to their table on the far reaches of the room near the warmth of the fire, and they saw Wish-Wash go to the bar and shake Malachy's hand. Then Malachy pointed to a door beside the bar and Wish-Wash walked towards it.

"Where's he going?" the Mayor said.

"He must want a word in private," Oodles said.

"What about?"

"How would I know!"

The Mayor locked his fingers on the table, and sighed. "There is a silver lining to me losing the use of my gold card," he said. "That clod-hopper can't trick me into footing the bill for the castle renovation."

Oodles stared at him. "You need to give Wish-Wash more credit. He knows what Malachy is up to."

The Mayor closed his eyes and massaged his eyelids with his fingers. "I hope you're right. It wouldn't be the first time he's put his big foot in it though." He opened his eyes abruptly. "Please don't tell him the story behind these clothes. I'd never hear the end of it."

Wish-Wash emerged from the door at the side of the bar, and had a big smile as he approached the table and sat down.

"What was all that about, old son?" Oodles asked.

Wish-Wash put a finger to the side of his nose.

The Mayor did that lifting-his-eyes-towards-the-sky thing again. Anyone would think he thought God was in a room on the next storey of the pub. "Don't tell us it was about the castle renovation?"

"OK, I won't tell you."

"Oh, for goodness sake! It was, wasn't it?"

"That's for me to know and for you to find out." Wish-Wash looked from drink to drink and the empty space in front of him. "Have you ordered your food, too?"

"We didn't think you'd be here so soon," the Mayor said. "It must have been a very quick email for a change."

Wish-Wash frowned. "There wasn't much to write. I told Moose the honey hadn't worked, but I could definitely hear it, so what should I do now?"

Oodles wondered if the time had come to set Wish-Wash straight. But it just wouldn't be right with the Mayor there. Wish-Wash didn't deserve that.

But what Wish-Wash said next gave him hope the big man might work it out for himself.

"I saw those kids near the bottom of the stairs when I was leaving the B&B," he said.

"Really," Oodles said, looking up smiling. "Were they with that runaway dog?"

"How did you know?"

"Educated guess. They were probably looking for a new hiding spot for it."

"Why? Cathleen and Shamus said they couldn't find the old hiding spot, so it must have been a goodie."

"Good point," Oodles said. "They were probably just taking it out then for fresh air and a pee."

"Do you reckon they were hiding it inside the building?"

"Dunno. What do you think?"

Wish-Wash stared into the middle-distance. "Yeah, you might be right."

Oodles let that thought percolate, then said: "What kind of dog was it?"

"Oh, you know I'm no good at dog breeds, cobber." Wish-Wash thought some more. "Bigger than a poodle, smaller than a great dane."

"About the same height as a Tasmanian Tiger?" Oodles prompted him.

Wish-Wash brightened. "Yeah, I suppose it was."

Oodles was thinking: *Wait for it, wait for it, any time now.*

But the Mayor spoiled the moment. "Nobody cares what breed it is," he said. "Shouldn't you order, Bert, before the kitchen closes?"

"Yeah, I suppose I should. What are you blokes having?" He looked at the blackboard on the wall.

"I couldn't look past the seafood chowder," Oodles said. "James could only come at the sandwiches."

"You paid for his? Or is he washing dishes?"

The Mayor exhaled noisily. "Clarence isn't as mean as you, Bert."

"Are you calling me mean? Does that mean you don't want another lemonade?"

"No, thank you. I've still got half mine left."

"Oodles?"

"Wouldn't say no." Oodles drained the rest of his pint of stout and slammed down the empty glass. "Same again."

"You sure? Will you be sober enough to drive us to the cemetery?"

"When?"

"After lunch."

"Why are we going to the cemetery?" Oodles said.

"Yes, why?" the Mayor said.

Wish-Wash rolled his eyes. "It's one of the reasons we're here. Family research. Hello?" He spoke above the crackle of the log. "You heard the bloke at the DNA office. The graveyard is a good place to start." He looked at the other faces. "Why do you think I got changed? I didn't want to show anyone up by wearing my green suit."

"I don't think the dead people would mind, Bert," the Mayor said.

"I was talking about you two," Wish-Wash said.

"What's wrong with these overalls?" Oodles looked at the Mayor. "Anyone would think they had dried fish guts on the sleeves?"

But this went right over Wish-Wash's head. "I wouldn't rule it out with all the trout you've caught." He sniffed the air. "It would explain that fishy smell."

He got up and went to the bar.

The Mayor waved a finger at Oodles. "Did you have to say that?"

"You know he'll find out sooner or later."

"If he does we'll know who told him."

The Mayor was wrong about that. Wish-Wash returned from the bar laughing. "Malachy and Conn have just been telling me about your wardrobe *malfunction*, Jimbo." *Hee-haw, hee-haw.* "I couldn't have planned it better myself."

The Mayor was very unimpressed with his sandwiches. He said the bread was stale and the ham tasted funny.

Oodles was delighted as usual with his seafood chowder.

But Wish-Wash looked the happiest as he tucked into his lamb roast. As usual, he spoke with his mouth full. "Malachy said this meat only came in this morning. Beautiful."

THIRTY-NINE
DUBHEASA O'DWYER GETS A VISITOR

Wish-Wash was miffed they didn't have flowers to take to the graveyard. But he needn't have worried.

It's a good thing Oodles had second thoughts about whether he might have been over the limit. They left the car where it was parked outside the B&B and walked to the cemetery, and if he had driven they might not have even seen the park on the way.

Not a lot actually blooms in Donegal in mid-winter but they collected the flowers were on offer in the park.

The Mayor looked down at his posey. "I feel silly."

"How do you think I feel?" Oodles said. "At least you two blokes will probably have relatives buried there, which means you can place your flowers on their graves. I'll be hobbling around the cemetery playing eenie-meeney-miney-mo."

The cemetery was on a hill next to the primary school.

After crossing the road, they all found a piece of stone fence to lean on to catch their breath and have a gander. It was dark overhead but the rain was holding off again.

"Why would they build a school next to a graveyard?" Oodles was puffing.

"Might have been the other way round," Wish-Wash said. "The school might have been here first."

"You're kidding me." Oodles raised his walking stick and pointed with it. "Look at the condition of some of those gravestones. They've been there a long time!"

"I think they've hit on a good idea," the Mayor said. "But that shouldn't surprise you because you'd know I was once up to my eyeballs in the finer points of town-planning."

"Design many cemeteries, did you?" Wish-Wash said.

"You know I didn't, Bert. But my ancestors probably played a part in the planning of the Windy Mountain cemetery." He looked at Oodles. "Even the Roman Catholic section."

"Oh, I get it," Oodles started tapping towards the gate. "That skill has been passed down in the genes."

The Mayor followed him. "You can laugh, Clarence. But consider this. Having a cemetery next door gives the kids looking out the window something to aspire to."

"What? Death?" Oodles said.

"Well, yes, there is that. They've got to learn that we all have to go sometime," the Mayor said. "But I didn't mean that. What I meant is a lot of high-achievers are probably buried in this graveyard. Doctors. Lawyers. Judges. Mayors."

Wish-Wash's eyes lit up. "Hey, perhaps you have a family mausoleum here we can leave you at?"

"Oh, very droll, Bert. Trust you to make light of this. What you're missing in your flippancy is that this graveyard is actually an excellent resource for the school. Just imagine the fun excursions they could have here."

Wish-Wash was wrong about the Northans having their own mausoleum.

The family did seem to have its own little section for plots though. It was steeper and more rocky, and the headstones weren't as big and grand as the ones on the Willson graves in the posh section.

The rain continued to hold off, which meant they were able to study the gravestones long enough to work out the writing — except for the really old ones the wind and rain had eroded over the years.

Oodles was correct. He couldn't find anyone called Noodle among all those graves.

He had no idea who Dubheasa O'Dwyer was but he doffed his cap when he placed the flowers on her grave. She had been dead so long, it looked like she hadn't had flowers for a very long time.

FORTY
VINEGAR

WISH-WASH WAS BALANCING the laptop on his thighs when Oodles woke up around 6am and looked over at the big man's bed. He didn't look happy.

"What's the matter, old son?"

"I just don't get it." Wish-Wash leaned back on the pillow wedged against the bed-head, stretched out his hands and locked his fingers. "I hate to say it but I'm beginning to think the Mayor's right. Moose is having a joke at my expense."

"He replied to your email?"

Wish-Wash nodded.

"And?"

"All he says is *try vinegar*."

"Vinegar?"

"That's what he says."

"Does he give any other instructions? Soak string in it? Load it into a tranquilliser gun? Anything?"

Wish-Wash shook his head. "No, just *try vinegar.*"

"What are you going to do?"

Wish-Wash cracked his knuckles. "I've been sitting here thinking about it. He's trying to make a fool out of me, isn't he? I can imagine him laughing every time he gets an email from me. *He actually tried honey. Ha-dee-ha-ha.*" He gave a pained look. "Why would he do that? I thought we were friends?"

"Don't be so quick to judge him," Oodles said. "We don't know what's going on at the museum — only that something is. Heard back from young Rod yet?"

Wish-Wash shook his head.

"There has got to be a reason for that, too," Oodles said. "He was very good taking us all the way to the airport and he wants you to go and live with him. This is uncharacteristic, wouldn't you agree?"

"Hard to say. Seems like I'm the only reliable one in the family. If Moose doesn't want to share the credit for catching that Tasmanian Tiger, fine. I'll wait a few hours then send back an email saying the vinegar didn't work either. Give him another reason to laugh. But don't expect me to give up. I'll figure out a way."

"You sure about this, old son?" Oodles's speech slowed down. "You might have been mistaken with what you saw?"

Wish-Wash fixed his eyes on him. "Oh, thanks a lot. Now you don't believe in me either."

Oodles put both palms up. "I didn't say that! But do you really want to wake James by raising your voice? I just think you should consider all the options."

"Fine. You'll be sorry, too, when I become rich and famous. What did Moose say? *Finding a Tasmanian Tiger in Ireland has got to be worth a million bucks.*"

His voice rose even louder. "And it's about time Jimbo was awake anyway."

With that, Wish-Wash put the laptop down by the side of his bed, rolled out and stomped into the bathroom.

Oodles watched the little Cherokee Indians disappear through the door and the Mayor lifted his head wondering what was going on.

When Wish-Wash re-emerged 10 minutes later, the Mayor was still rubbing his eyes. This meant only Oodles saw Wish-Wash had something secreted under those pyjamas.

————

Exactly what was hidden was revealed when the Mayor had his turn in the bathroom.

He had only been in there a minute, when he screamed: "WHERE HAS IT GONE?"

"Where's what gone?" Wish-Wash yelled back.

"SOMEONE'S MOVED MY TOOTHBRUSH."

"Wasn't me," Oodles shouted.

"The spare toothbrush I lent you?" Wish-Wash shouted. "You probably left it somewhere and forgot where."

The Mayor opened the door and peered out. "What are you insinuating? That I'm losing my faculties?"

"Nothing to be ashamed of at your age," Wish-Wash said.

"My age! Might I remind you I'm a year younger than you!" He pointed to Oodles. "And I'm three years younger than you, Clarence."

Wish-Wash came back at him. "But we haven't mislaid our toothbrushes."

The Mayor slammed the door.

Oodles looked at Wish-Wash and lowered his voice. "You took it, didn't you?"

Wish-Wash removed the sparkly red toothbrush from beneath his pyjama top. "I told you I'd get his DNA somehow. But it's not really theft because it was mine anyway. Guess where I bought it?"

Oodles squeezed his eyes shut. "So not only is it second-hand, you might have further contaminated the sample with your own sweat now."

"Who sweats in this weather?" Wish-Wash examined the toothbrush. "I'm more worried I might have accidentally brushed my teeth with this?"

Oodles pulled a face. "You didn't?"

"Hard to say. It might have been yours I accidentally used."

Oodles's eyes widened.

"It's not my fault," Wish-Wash said. "All our toothbrushes look so much alike."

"They're all different blinking colours!"

"It's not my fault I'm a bit flaming colour-blind?"

"Strewth," Oodles said. "Last time I suggested that, you denied it."

"I only have trouble in low light. And it's dark in that bathroom unless you turn the shaving light on."

"For Gawdsake, why don't you then?"

Wish-Wash stroked his grey beard. "Obviously, I don't need to now."

The noise of crashing drawers and cabinet doors told Oodles that James Northan was getting increasingly frustrated.

"Strewth, old son, how to you propose getting hold of Conn Northan's toothbrush."

Wish-Wash smiled. "I don't have to. That's what my quiet word with Malachy was all about yesterday. He's going to put one of Conn's unwashed pint glasses aside for me."

———

The Mayor emerged from the bathroom wearing different underpants.

"What happened to your red ones?" Wish-Wash said.

"I got two pairs from the caravan, remember?" the Mayor hissed. The ones he was wearing were silk boxers, mainly yellow with green dragons.

"Oh, I like those ones," Wish-Wash said. "Feel free to leave them to me in your will."

The Mayor glared at him as he pulled on his jeans.

"Did you find your toothbrush?" Wish-Wash sat on the side of the bed and wriggled into his stretchy tracky-dackies.

"No, I did not. Someone's obviously come in here and stolen it."

"Who would do that?"

The Mayor scoffed. "There are too many people to point the finger at in this village. Everyone seems to be on the take."

Oodles was sitting on his bed tying his shoelaces, but looked up. "That's a bit harsh, old son! Cathleen seems honest enough."

"You think? We know she has a key to this room."

"And you think she came in here when weren't here and stole your toothbrush," Oodles said.

"Her or her husband. We know Shamus associates with the riff-raff at the drinking establishment."

Wish-Wash put on his angry face. "Are you calling my cousin dodgy?"

The Mayor gave a mock laugh. "Ha, Malachy is the kingpin. When are you going to realise he's trying to extort money from you to do those castle renovations?"

"Trying it on doesn't make him a crook," Wish-Wash said. "Don't tell me you've never tried to wack it over someone to get your way."

"That's quite different. And *wack it over* isn't a phrase I would use. I prefer *outwit*."

Oodles raised his open hands. "This conversation isn't getting us anywhere."

"You're right, Clarence." The Mayor sighed as he inspected the sleeves of his sweater. "I'll need to buy a new toothbrush. My mouth tastes like the bottom of a budgie cage."

"Lick many budgie cages, do you?" Wish-Wash said.

"You know what I mean? I hate starting the day without cleaning my teeth."

"I see one problem," Oodles said. "Where would you go to buy a toothbrush in this village? I haven't seen one shop."

Wish-Wash's face lit up. "Perhaps the pub sells them?"

"What pub sells toothbrushes?" Oodles said.

"You haven't been in the room behind the bar," Wish-Wash said. "I saw all kinds of grocery items on the shelf. My cousin must sell other items under the counter. I thought it was odd the first time we walked in and a bloke passed us on the way out carrying a loaf of bread. Who takes a French stick into a pub?"

"You think they fell off the back of a truck, old son?"

"I didn't ask."

"Oh, for goodness sake!" the Mayor said, as he pulled on a sock. "No way am I buying from him. Do you think I want to be found in possession of a stolen toothbrush?"

Wish-Wash bristled. "Malachy is a legitimate businessman. He's not likely to pass on stolen goods. You, on the other hand, think stealing potatoes is OK."

"Seriously, Bert?" The Mayor was now rubbing hair cream into his scalp. "You keep failing to grasp the fact it was my ancestor who stole those potatoes, not me."

"Yeah, but it was stolen from my family, so that's seven things you owe me now."

"Seven?" The Mayor stopped rubbing.

Wish-Wash counted them out on his fingers. "One potato, two potatoes, three potatoes, one three-piece suit, one shirt, one tie, and one pair of patented leather shoes."

FORTY-ONE
A BRUSH WITH TOOTHBRUSHES

No wonder the Mayor's mouth tasted like the bottom of a budgie cage? He skipped the full Irish breakfast again and hit the breakfast bar once more. The muesli contained enough seeds and grains to make your average budgie chirp all day.

"If you refuse to try the pub, James, that leaves us with no choice," Oodles said. "We'll have to drive over to Letterkenny again."

"Again!" the Mayor said.

"What's the big deal?" Wish-Wash said. "You've only been there twice. Me and Oodles had to go three times."

"Right! Once because you *forgot* me!"

"It's your own damn fault for being so quiet in the back seat," Wish-Wash said.

"What should I have done when I wasn't there? Spoken up?"

Wish-Wash crossed his arms and continued chewing his black pudding. Then he gave the Mayor a spray. Literally. "I still can't see why you can't check out the pub first? It's going to spoil our day's plans if we have to waste time driving to Letterkenny."

The plan had been to drive to some more villages along the Wild Atlantic Way. Wish-Wash wanted to explore some more graveyards, hoping to uncover some more family connections. He had tracked down the Willsons, the Whishs had to have come from somewhere.

Oodles's big wish was they'd stumble on a nice pub so he could compare seafood chowders.

The Mayor hadn't been keen about either destination, but the idea of Letterkenny seemed to thrill him even less.

The Mayor laid his spoon in his empty bowl. "It occurs to me we have another alternative."

"We're listening," Wish-Wash said, chewing a large slice of bacon.

"Let me have my computer back and I'll buy them online. I'll get new toothbrushes for all of us!"

"Don't be stupid," Wish-Wash said. "I've never heard of anyone buying toothbrushes over the inter-web. What happens? Do they email them to you?"

"Now who's being stupid? They are mailed out. They'd be here in a day or two."

Wish-Wash gave him another spray. Egg this time. "You must think I'm really thick, Jimbo? No way are you getting your grubby hands on *my* computer. And even if I let you, you have no way to pay now your credit card has been cancelled. Or do you know a site that gives away free toothbrushes?"

The Mayor shook his head. "For your information, I won't need a credit card. I happen to have a PayPal account."

"Oh, nice try." Wish-Wash leaned back in his chair and started laughing. "Pity I have no idea what you're talking about? The answer is still no."

———

Once he had used his serviette to wipe the flecks of egg, black pudding, and saliva from his blue-grey jumper, the Mayor agreed to give the pub a try after all.

"I'm warning you though — if the toothbrush is not in a sealed package, I'm not touching it."

"Fair enough." Wish-Wash looked out the window and rubbed his hands together. "It looks like a nice day to explore some more graveyards."

The Mayor looked out to the same black clouds. "It's going to rain!"

"The trouble with you is you're not optimistic enough, Jimbo," Wish-Wash said.

"That's because I'm a realist. It's going to rain, like it always rains here."

"What if I told you I had actually seen packs of toothbrushes on Malachy's shelves. Would that improve your optimism?"

"You've actually seen them?"

"I'm 99 per cent sure I have."

"Not 100 per cent?"

"No such thing as a dead-certainty!" Wish-Wash said. "A bloke's always got to leave himself a way out. What if there has been a run on toothbrushes and Malachy's sold out."

"How many toothbrushes do you think you saw?"

Wish-Wash looked out of the window and thought. "Hmm, at least a dozen."

The Mayor smiled. "There'd still be plenty left then, even if there has been a run on them. I doubt there are that many people in this village into dental hygiene."

———

Conn Northan's tooth-depleted smile added weight to this theory. He and Paddy O'Hare turned when the three old men entered the pub. "Oh, it's just you fellas," Conn said. "Make sure you close that fecking door, I'm foundered."

"You must live here?" the Mayor said.

"Aye, we both live upstairs." He laughed. "We have a long commute, don't we Paddy?"

Paddy O'Hare was wearing the grey suit again. Oodles wondered how the Mayor stopped himself growling like a rottweiler.

Instead, The Mayor cleared his throat. "Is Wish-Wash's cousin around?"

"He hasn't come down yet. Can we help?"

"I doubt it," the Mayor said.

"We often open the bar when Malachy's had a big night, like."

Oodles frowned. "Was last night a big night for him?"

"Aye. Another football international," Conn said.

"Ireland again?"

"No, Lithuania. This pub has Sky."

Wish-Wash came out with it. "We want to buy some toothbrushes."

"Toothbrushes? Here?"

Wish-Wash pointed. "I'm pretty sure I saw them on the shelf in that room there."

"Really? I'll check." Conn got off his barstool and headed to the door. He took a key out of his trousers pocket, unlocked the door and went in.

Wish-Wash slapped Paddy on the back. "So how's that new suit going for you?"

"Dis?" Paddy looked downwards. "I wish the trousers weren't so tight. I need more ball room. I'm starting to tink I ought to have never swapped my clothes for dis. I was very fond especially of the yellow boxer shorts with the green dragons."

The Mayor's face crumpled.

Conn returned with a small box.

"I couldn't find any toothbrushes, sorry. Are these any good to you?" He put the box on the counter and pulled out a tube of toothpaste.

The Mayor turned to Wish-Wash. "You were 99 per cent sure, eh?"

"The branding on the box threw me. Who knew that mob makes toothpaste as well as toothbrushes?"

"Oh, for goodness sake!"

Both their eyes turned when Conn started clearing his throat. "I can let you have the lot for 20 euros. You didn't buy them here, OK?"

FORTY-TWO
RED, WHITE AND BLUE

THE MAYOR'S inclination was to say no. But Wish-Wash pulled his wallet out immediately.

"So we're off to Letterkenny after all," the Mayor said as they headed outside to the car.

"Pig's arse!" Wish-Wash was carrying the box under his arm. "Who needs a toothbrush when you have enough toothpaste you can just smear it on with your fingers?"

"That's gross," the Mayor said.

"If you don't like that, you can smear your share on any older gravestones we find to see if it makes the inscriptions any easier to read."

The Mayor stopped on the footpath and put a hand to his mouth. "That'd be desecration!"

Wish-Wash turned and smiled. "If anyone sees us, we'll just claim you're giving the stones a clean." When he saw the look on the Mayor's face, he said, "What? It's not like the long deceased are going to worry about the smell of peppermint. If anything it'll give them a nice minty glow."

Oodles took no convincing. He was done with Letterkenny and he was keen to compare seafood chowders.

They did find a shop that sold toothbrushes that did satisfy the Mayor's insistence they come in sealed packaging. They bought a red one, a blue one and a white one.

They also found a nice pub for lunch, which coincided with the heaviest downpour of the day.

And old graveyards weren't in short supply.

None of them furthered Wish-Wash's knowledge, however, and none of the toothpaste was needed.

They were back at the B&B by late afternoon.

Wish-Wash didn't even bother checking on the captive in the kitchen.

He sent his email saying the vinegar hadn't worked, then settled into a science fiction novel he had brought in his suitcase. Oodles had put the proper glasses case on Wish-Wash's bedside table but the big man said he didn't need them. "I think your mate Goody mucked up my prescription. Those specs make me feel wonky."

Oodles buried his head into a novel on his e-reader.

The Mayor started the second lap of his *Reader's Digest*.

FORTY-THREE
SAUCER OF MILK

Wish-Wash looked like he was trying to stave off a headache when Oodles woke up just before 6am.

The big man was propped up on his pillow again and was pinching the bridge of his nose.

The laptop was lying lid open on the floor.

"Are you all right, old mate?" Oodles whispered.

Wish-Wash removed his hand and glanced over. "Not really," he said flatly. "I never expected Moose to treat me like this."

Oodles ran a hand through his thinning hair. "What's he done now?"

"I don't understand it. Moose and I go way back. He stood by me when I was the target of all kinds of ridicule."

"Is his latest email worse than the one suggesting you trap the Tasmanian Tiger with vinegar?" Oodles asked.

"Read it for yourself."

Wish-Wash slid the laptop across the floor.

It stopped midway, so Oodles had to get out of bed to fetch it. He sat down on the side of the bed and read it.

When he looked up, Wish-Wash was still pinching his nose, and Oodles now knew why.

This email went beyond ridicule. This was the kind of taunt Wish-Wash had copped time after time after his alleged sighting of a Tasmanian Tiger in 1967.

How could Moose be so cruel?

He glanced back down to the email.

"Try sliding a saucer of milk under the door. Then call out: 'Here Kitty, Kitty, Kitty.'"

———

Oodles herded Wish-Wash and a reluctant Mayor down to the breakfast room about 6.30am.

Cathleen was just putting out the cereal and fruit when they walked in, and she jumped when she heard them come in behind her.

"Jesus Mary and Joseph." She turned and clutched her chest. "I only just beat you here. I won't have anyting cooked for at least another half hour."

"We're in no hurry," Oodles said, and she disappeared back through the swinging doors.

The Mayor made a beeline for the budgie food again.

"Why did you tell her that?" Wish-Wash said. "Sooner we have breakfast, sooner I can go check on that Tasmanian Tiger."

"What's another half an hour going to matter? If a Tasmanian Tiger really is in the guest kitchen, it's not going anywhere."

"*If?* You used to have faith in me, cobber?"

"I didn't mean it like that?"

Wish-Wash sighed. "I'm going to show everyone — the Mayor, you and especially Moose. I should have done this all those years ago. I was so close to that Tasmanian Tiger in the bus shelter I could have reached out, grabbed its tail and held it until help arrived."

"Strewth, you're not planning to do anything stupid, are you?"

"Not stupid. Brave. I'm no chicken. I'm going in."

Wish-Wash didn't even wait for Cathleen to return to take their order. He stood up abruptly and headed towards the door, with Oodles in close pursuit.

The Mayor was returning to their table with his bowl and almost tipped it. "Where are you going?"

"Back in a minute," Oodles said, doing a fast hobble across the room on his walking stick.

———

'Noooooo," Wish-Wash cried as he approached the kitchen and saw the door was open. "It's escaped."

FORTY-FOUR
TEARS #1

OODLES WATCHED Wish-Wash crumple to the floor and start sobbing. "This is the story of my life. I let him get away again."

Oodles had never seen him cry before. He leaned down and patted him on the back of his bright orange, green and white Christmas jumper. "Let it out, old son. You weren't the one who opened the door."

Wish-Wash looked up to him with watery eyes. "I'll never hear the end of it from Jimbo."

"I won't tell him." This certainly wasn't the time to come clean with his suspicions, not when Wish-Wash was in this state. "We can pretend this whole thing never happened. What do you say? He'll think he had a bad dream or he's going senile. His word against ours. More torture!"

This brightened up Wish-Wash immediately but he switched to a look of concern just as quickly. "What about Moose?"

"What about him?"

"He's already laughing at me — and he doesn't even know about t-t-his."

"Come on." Oodles patted Wish-Wash's shoulder. Why he was

wearing a Christmas jumper with a reindeer on the front was a mystery. He probably thought the orange, green and white went well with his green and swirly orange tracky-dackies. "Buck up. Moose doesn't have to know either. He probably thinks you're the one trying to kid him, so we'll keep it that way. The only way he's ever like to find out what really happened is by comparing notes with James. But what are the chances of that happening when they hate each other."

Wish-Wash got to his knees and pulled out another white handkerchief that had someone else's monogram. "You sure?" He blew his nose like a foghorn.

"Sure I'm sure," Oodles said. "What you need is a holiday away from this holiday. Can we bring our trip to Paris forward?"

Wish-Wash looked up at him blankly. "What trip to Paris?"

"Disneyland Paris. Hello?"

"Oh, that? Didn't you hear them at Letterkenny? The DNA people said there was no money in their budget for that. They said we'd have to finance our own side trip."

Oodles scratched his head.

"Too bad we haven't got that kind of money," Wish-Wash said.

"Hmm, don't give up on your dream." Oodles offered a hand. "Come on, let's get you up. James will be wondering where we are."

———

The Mayor was just starting to tuck into his bowl when Wish-Wash and Oodles came through the door. It probably wasn't his first bowl though.

"Well?" the Mayor said.

"Well, what?" Oodles replied, as he sat down.

The Mayor burst out laughing. "I was expecting you to drag a Tasmanian Tiger through that door."

Oodles looked at him deadpan. "Why would you think that?"

The Mayor faltered. "I thought you were going to the guest kitchen?"

"The guest kitchen?" Oodles frowned. "You think we were going to make our own Irish breakfasts? What's got into you to make you so funny this morning?"

"Bert has been saying for days a Tasmanian Tiger is locked in there."

Oodles gave him a sympathetic look. "Are you feeling all right, James? The stress of this trip isn't getting to you, is it?"

"I'm perfectly well, thank you. Even Cathleen saw you had left the room. Explain that!"

"Easy. We didn't want to smoke inside."

"Smoke?" The Mayor looked at both their faces. "I thought you had both given up the cancer sticks?"

"We lapsed."

"Both of you?"

"We made a pact. Ever see that movie about Butch Cassidy and the Sundance Kid? We jumped together."

The Mayor looked back at Wish-Wash. "How come Bert has red eyes?"

"He's not used to the smoke any more," Oodles said quickly.

The Mayor sniffed. "How come I can't smell smoke residue?"

Oodles found his answer out the window when he saw dark clouds moving across the sky at the rate of knots. "The strong wind was blowing the smoke away from us."

"Ah, but Bert still got smoke in his eyes?"

"It's one of the downsides of being tall. The rising smoke must have just caught him."

The Mayor looked up when Cathleen came through the swinging door with her order book. "You're back! Two full Irish breakfasts?"

When she had retreated with their order, the Mayor said: "So did you spend anytime thinking on this long *cigarette break* of yours about what's next on this trip?"

"We did actually. Trouble is we don't know how to finance our side trip to Paris."

"What?" The Mayor looked from face to face. "I thought that was already paid for?"

"Turns out it's not."

"Don't look at me? Even if my credit card hadn't been cancelled, I've got no interest in Disneyland whatsoever."

"I thought you wanted to visit The Louvre?"

The Mayor looked into the middle distance and obviously liked what he was imagining, then he sighed. "Lucky I've already been there."

"They've probably hung a new version of the Mona Lisa." When the Mayor glared at him, Oodles added. "It's possible, isn't it? Claude Monet did a whole series on water lilies from different angles. Perhaps they've found the Picasso version with five noses?"

The Mayor tapped on the table. "It's academic anyway. I've got eight more days before I can pick up my new credit card in Dublin. Three days later, we'll be on the flight home."

Oodles tried another tack. "You did mention yesterday you have a PayPal account. We'd pay you back, of course. What if — and I'm not saying this would happen — Wish-Wash's computer turned out to be *your* computer. Would that help?"

Wish-Wash glared at Oodles. "We've been through this. The airline gave me that laptop."

"Yes, but what good is it to you now, old son?"

"You never know. Rod might reply to my email."

The Mayor waved a finger. "Nice try. I know what you two are up to. Good cop, bad cop. But I'm not sure I want that old computer back anyway. I plan to upgrade to a much better one in Dublin. And another thing. I have a very small limit with PayPal. Yes, it's good for buying toothbrushes — but trips to Paris? Forget it."

"Can't you do bank transfers on your phone?"

"Don't you think I might have mentioned that if I could? For goodness sake, I never do any financial dealings on my phone. You might as well wave large wads of cash in front of mobs of thieves."

The two Irish breakfasts arrived and everyone ate quietly.

The Mayor finally broke the silence. "So what's on the agenda to see today? More ghastly cemeteries?"

Oodles had his mouthful and he shook his head.

He swallowed. "If it's OK with you blokes, I'd just like to take it easy today. Can we find a nice spot by the sea and just read our books?"

"There's that bench up near my castle." Wish-Wash addressed the Mayor. "The one you sat on, Jimbo?"

"And what am I going to read?" the Mayor complained. "I can almost recite that *Reader's Digest* off by heart."

"I've finished one of my books," Wish-Wash said. "You can have that."

"One of your books? Science fiction!"

Wish-Wash scoffed."You can learn a lot from sci-fi. Some of that stuff comes true."

"And a lot of it doesn't. Exhibit One: they found neither Uncle Martin nor little green men on Mars."

"Please yourself." Wish-Wash sprayed more flecks of egg. "You can look at that fancy under-used phone of yours then. If you get sick of that you can read about Joe's sphincter again, which is probably right up your alley."

FORTY-FIVE
TEARS #2

THEY SAW it as soon as they neared the castle. A large cardboard box sat out the front.

Oodles parked the car, and looked over. "What do you think it is?"

"Oh Lordy," came the distraught voice from the back seat. "I had forgotten all about it with everything that's been happening."

Wish-Wash looked towards the back seat. "Don't tell me someone's sent you a care package, Jimbo? Why did they leave it here?"

"This is the address I provided," the Mayor said. "How was I to know we wouldn't be living here?"

"If there's any chocolate digestive biscuits in that box, we want a share of them, don't we Oodles? Think of it as rent for using this address. I might even accept biscuits in lieu of potatoes."

"You're out of luck then because it's not the kind of package you think it is."

He was right about that.

Wish-Wash and Oodles followed him and watched him open the box and lift Colonel Richard Northan's large bronze head out.

———

The Mayor crumpled to the road and started sobbing as the head bounced away from him across the carpark. *Clang, clang, clang.*

Oodles had never seen James Northan cry before either, so it was quite surreal. He leaned down and patted him on the back of his woollen sweater. "How on earth did that thing get here?"

The Mayor looked up to him with watery eyes. "I asked Rod to send it airfreight."

"You were *that* desperate to bury it in the soil of his homeland!"

The Mayor doubled over again and his body trembled with new sobs. "I thought there would be spikes!"

"What?"

The Mayor came up for air and blubbered. "How was I to know it'd only be half a castle — and have no spikes whatsoever?"

Oodles looked around at Wish-Wash who was smiling like he had just won the lottery. Oodles guessed he had never seen the Mayor crying before either but he was really enjoying the spectacle.

"So you lied to us?" Oodles said. "You had no intention of burying the head?"

The Mayor wiped the snot from his nose with a hand. "I wanted the crows to pick out his eyeballs," he hissed. "I wanted his head to wither away up there. I wanted Robert Northan to feel just some of the humiliation he brought upon our family."

Wish-Wash broke in. "You of all people should know that head looks nothing like your great, great, great grandfather! Didn't you have it modelled on Captain Blood?"

"It's the principle. He disgraced our good name."

"How? By founding Windy Mountain?"

"By being a mere convict. An Irishman. Not an English nobleman. Not a colonel in the British army." James Northan got to his knees and pointed up the tower wall. "He deserved to be made an example of."

"Strewth, old son," Oodles said. "Did you think this through? Even if there had been spikes, how did you plan to get the head up there?"

The Mayor shook his head, sending a spray of tear-droplets flying. "I was soooo wrong. I thought you and Bert would come around."

Oodles knew what that was about. When Oodles worked in the works depot at the Windy Mountain Council and James really was the Mayor, he was frequently tasked cleaning bird poop from the top of Colonel Northan's head. This involved resting a ladder on the sculpture, which depicted Colonel Richard Northan astride rearing horse, and climbing way up to the top. Now he was 85, though, and hadn't actually brought a ladder with him, he wasn't quite sure what the Mayor had had in mind. Perhaps he had thought Oodles could stand on Wish-Wash's shoulders?

"But you didn't let up, did you?" the Mayor said. "You've been horrible to me this whole time."

Oodles and Wish-Wash looked at each other.

"But I deserved this, didn't I? I've been so horrible to both of you over the years." The Mayor bowed his head, and tears and snot dripped on to the ground. "Can you ever forgive me?"

Wish-Wash stared down. "What did you just say?"

The Mayor looked up at him and used both hands to wipe his cheeks. "I suppose I'm asking for forgiveness."

Wish-Wash patted him on the shoulder. "Of course we forgive you, Jimbo. You just need a holiday away from this holiday."

———

They buried the head in a shallow grave overlooking the sea.

The Mayor did most of the digging with his bare hands; well, it was *his* head, after all, and Oodles and Wish-Wash would have helped more if shovels had been on hand.

For his part, Wish-Wash said some nice words over the grave. "Ashes to ashes, rust to rust."

Then they settled down on the park bench, just like old times.

Wish-Wash cleared his throat. "Since we're coming clean, Jimbo, I have a confession of my own."

"What?" The Mayor looked sideways at him.

"That laptop *is* yours."

"I know. But I meant what I said. Keep it. When we get to Dublin, I'm going to buy the latest model."

"But I insist you take it back. I've come around to Oodles's way of thinking."

"I thought that was just an act?"

"No way! He was never speaking for me." He turned his head to Oodles, who was sitting on the other end. "Were you, cobber?"

Then he turned back the other way to the Mayor. "Maybe now you'll be able to email your daughter and ask her to transfer some money to you so you can pay for our side trip."

"Maddie? What makes you think she'd send me money? And how would she even get it to me?"

"Don't you do internet banking on the laptop?"

The Mayor shook his head. "I'm still getting over the fact they don't stamp passbooks at the bank any more. I certainly don't trust internet banking."

"Christ, what *do* you use the computer for?"

The Mayor screwed up his face. "I told you: email, I subscribe to some news sites and I like to keep abreast with what's happening on my share portfolio."

Wish-Wash slapped his forehead. "Of course! How much is that worth?"

The Mayor stared. "That is the height of rudeness. It's none of your business what it's worth."

"Fair enough. I'll rephrase that. All we need is enough to cover our trip to Disneyland Paris. Can you manage that?"

"I don't even want to go to Disneyland."

"You don't have to. We can drop you at the Loo."

"It's called the Louvre." The Mayor raised a palm. "You're forgetting one thing. Even if I get my accountant to sell the shares to finance this little jolly, I don't do internet banking. Thus, he has no way of getting the money to me."

"Get him to pay for it all at his end and email us the tickets."

"He's an accountant, not a travel agent!"

"Since when did you start worrying about asking employees to do things outside their wheelhouse?"

FORTY-SIX
THE BROWN PAPER BAG

WISH-WASH SAID he wanted to send one last email and then he'd hand over the computer.

The Mayor said he'd think about it over lunch.

"So? Seafood chowder at the pub?" Wish-Wash said.

The Mayor groaned. "Surely there's another dining option?" He turned to Oodles. "What about that hotel we went to yesterday, Clarence?"

"That's an hour away," Oodles said. "I'm tired. You want to go there, you'll have to drive!"

The Mayor looked around at Wish-Wash. "Don't look at me," the man in the Christmas jumper said. "I told you: no way am I driving unlicensed. I need to uphold my family's spotless reputation."

The Mayor kept staring. "So how does Malachy fit into this untarnished dynasty?"

Wish-Wash held his gaze. "You can't blame a bloke for wanting to make ends meet."

"By selling stolen goods under the counter?"

"I hardly think a few loaves of hot bread and boxes of toothpaste make him Mr Big."

"He smokes behind the bar in defiance of the law!"

"Mr Cig maybe. Not Mr Big. But we've only seen him do that twice."

"We've only been here three days! And what about the castle? It's pretty obvious to me he wants you to foot the bill for the restoration, so he can then cash in on it."

"How?" Wish-Wash said.

"Didn't he say he's next in line to inherit it? *Oops, oh deary me, my 83-year-old cousin has lost his balance. He only went to the tower with me to inspect the finished work.*"

Wish-Wash shook his head. "I think you read too many crime books, Jimbo. But you're missing the point. As long as Malachy thinks I've actually got the money to pay for the work, it actually puts me in a position of power. It means he'll do my bidding until things begin."

"Your bidding? For what?"

"That's for me to know and for you to find out. Just don't tell him we've been up here this morning. That might give him the wrong idea."

"So when are you planning to tell him it's not actually going to happen?"

"Not today. If he asks, we've been looking at more graveyards, doing further family research."

When Oodles parked outside the B&B, Wish-Wash was holding a small brown paper bag when he got out of the car and they walked to the pub.

Malachy greeted them warmly when they walked in.

The Mayor's eyes fell on Shamus and Paddy O'Hare sitting side-by-side, two grey pinstripe suits in a row.

In his white-hot rage, he might not even have processed that Wish-Wash handed the brown paper bag over to Malachy, who then tucked it under the bar.

But Oodles knew the Mayor's DNA genetic sample had been handed over.

Wish-Wash had Malachy doing his bidding, all right. It was only a matter of time before the toothbrush and the pint glass were mailed to the DNA office.

Wish-Wash and Oodles both ordered the seafood chowder, and the Mayor ordered the lamb roast.

He was surprised when three seafood chowders turned up at the table. They had run out of lamb.

They went back to their B&B room after lunch, and the Mayor went for an early shower.

Oodles stood watching as Wish-Wash wrote his final email:

We couldn't slide the saucer of milk under the door because there isn't enough room.

Jimbo says he's had enough and is going in.

We'll keep you informed of developments.

FORTY-SEVEN

'ESSAYEZ-VOUS DE ME RENDRE STUPIDE?'

WHEN THE MAYOR came out dressed in a towel, the laptop was already on his bed.

"All yours." Wish-Wash handed him a pen and paper. "You might want to write down the new password. It's six digits long."

"Certainly." The Mayor sat down, his pen poised.

"Ready? One ... two ... three ... four ... five ... six." Wish-Wash looked over when he detected the lack of movement. "You're not even writing."

The Mayor looked up at him. "Is that it?"

"I didn't want to forget it."

The Mayor repeated the sequence slowly as if he hadn't believed his ears. "One ... two ... three ... four ... five ... six?"

"You've committed it to memory!" Wish-Wash sounded amazed. "Oh, you're good!"

"And you think that's secure, do you?"

"You never cracked it."

"I never tried to crack it, Bert! I told you: it's a very old computer. I don't even know how you talked me into taking it back."

"How else will you be able to sell your shares to finance our side trip?"

The Mayor rolled his eyes. "That's the only reason I agreed. I was thinking about it in the shower. I won't have to wait till Dublin. I can go clothes shopping in Paris."

Oodles lifted his eyes from his e-reader. "That's going to be hard without a credit card, old son."

"That's one of the reasons I pay Colin top remuneration. He's the kind of accountant who comes up with creative solutions."

"So you're not going to the art museum now?" Oodles said.

The Mayor shook his head. "As much as I feel in the need of cultural cleansing, I'm not going in a fisherman's woollen jumper and gumboots. I might as well borrow those orange and green pants you've got on."

Wish-Wash's face creased. "I'm not lending you these, not after you gave away Lambsie! You must be joking!"

"I am, actually. *Essayez-vous de me rendre stupide?*"

"Say that in English?"

"Really, Bert? How do you even plan to catch a taxi in Paris if you don't even have some elementary French?"

"Sign language?" Wish-Wash flashed the only signal in his repertoire. A rude one.

The Mayor looked unimpressed. "I'd better drop you two off, rather than vice-versa, then go on to the shop Colin organises? When you see me again, I'll be back to my debonair self." He looked down to the keyboard again and started tapping as he muttered: "Un, deux, trois, quatre, cinq, six. I don't believe it."

Oodles and Wish-Wash were both deep into their novels when The Mayor rubbed his hands together.

Oodles looked up from his bed. "Success?"

"Paris, here we come." The Mayor closed the lid and smiled as he stood up from the table. "I've sent a detailed email to Colin, which should be one of the first he opens when he logs in for the day. By the time we wake up tomorrow, it should all be done."

"So you were able to check your share portfolio then?" Oodles said.

"Shame to have to offload some of them, actually. They're doing awfully well."

"Sorry about that."

"Don't be. The more I think of it, the more excited I am. After I get myself fitted out with a couple of decent suits, I'm going to find a nice street cafe and sit down for coffee and croissants."

Wish-Wash looked up from his book."I wonder if they sell dagwood dogs at Disneyland Paris?"

"Oh, for heaven's sake," the Mayor said.

FORTY-EIGHT

'WOULDN'T IT HAVE BEEN CHEAPER TO BUY US A CUPPA IN THE WIND TUNNEL CAFE BACK HOME?'

THE MAYOR WAS right about his accountant. When he checked his email before breakfast, Colin had arranged business-class airfares for the three of them, three nights accommodation at a five-star hotel on the left bank of the River Seine, transfers, and some vouchers for James Northan to use in Paris.

"Strewth, first-class airfares, five-star hotel?" Oodles said. "That's very generous of you."

"Yes, it's costing a bomb," The Mayor said. "It's against my better judgement but Colin says it'll work out cheaper this way because I can claim it back as a business expense, you being my clients. I told you he was creative."

"Oh la la, we're your clients now?" Wish-Wash said. "Wouldn't it have been cheaper to buy us a cuppa in the Wind Tunnel Cafe back home?"

"Don't look a gift-horse in the mouth, Bert." The Mayor said. "I'm not about to question Colin. He's sent some documents through for you both to sign in Paris — to be witnessed by the hotel concierge to prove you were actually there."

"What kind of documents?" Wish-Wash said.

"Gobbledygook really. We don't want anyone in the tax office to actually understand it. I'll get a copy printed out for you. Cathleen must have a printer down in reception."

"When are we going?" Wish-Wash said.

"Tomorrow morning."

Wish-Wash looked at Oodles. "What time will we need to get up to make it to the airport in Dublin?"

"Didn't I say?" The Mayor said. "We catch a small plane from the airport near here and connect with an Aer Lingus flight in Dublin that will take us directly to Paris Charles de Gaulle Airport. It does the reverse coming back, which means we'll only have two or three days here before driving back to Dublin. I've also arranged for Colin to arrange an upgrade to business-class for me on our flight home." He rubbed his hands again.

FORTY-NINE
QUICK, DON'T LET HIM GET AWAY

Oodles was swinging his car keys in his free hand when they emerged from the B&B. They all had full stomachs fortified by hot tea, and came outside bracing for the cold.

When a man rugged up in a yellow, red and green tie-dyed jumper walked straight past them, they froze on the footpath!

They watched the culprit get into the driver's seat of a car a few vehicles down.

"Did you see that?" Wish-Wash gasped. "That bloke is wearing my jumper."

"So?" The Mayor said. "I've got two men in this village wearing my suits, but you don't hear me complaining."

The others looked at him.

The new Lambsie started his engine.

Wish-Wash turned again. "We can't let him get away," he cried.

Then he grabbed the keys from Oodles's hand, held on to his cap, and dashed for the driver's door of the hire car.

Oodles and The Mayor looked at each other as the car roared into life and Wish-Wash took off in a stutter of kangaroo hops.

He didn't get far. A marked Garda car appeared from a side street 30 yards down the road and blocked his path.

FIFTY
EN GARDA

When Wish-Wash walked back up the road about 20 minutes later, he was holding a piece of paper.

Oodles blew out steam into the cold air. "Not a fine?"

"Worse." Wish-Wash shivered. "It's an advisory about what will happen to me if I don't present my licence to the police station in Letterkenny within 24 hours." He unfolded the paper and paraphrased it. "Jail and/or a whopping big fine."

Wish-Wash handed the paper to Oodles and rubbed his cold hands together. "You'd think he would have cut me some slack when I told him I had incurred not so much as a parking ticket since I started driving."

"Strewth," Oodles said. "You lied about having a licence?"

"Not exactly," Wish-Wash said. "I just said I didn't have it on me, which was true."

"Oh, for goodness sake," the Mayor said.

Wish-Wash turned on him. "Don't you moan, Jimbo! This is all your fault. If you hadn't given away Lambsie we would never have had to go home so soon."

FIFTY-ONE
GET OUT WHILE YOU CAN

"WE CAN'T GO HOME NOW," the Mayor gasped as watched Wish-Wash lift one of the suitcases in the car boot. "What about the trip to Paris I've already paid for?"

Wish-Wash turned and waved a finger at him. "You should have thought about that before you gave away Lambsie. Consider yourself lucky I carried these two suitcases down here. Have you even packed yet?"

The Mayor folded his arms. "Even if I had something to pack, where would I pack it? And what if I insist on staying?"

"I don't think you understand the hot water we are in." Wish-Wash stretched out his hands and counted out on his fingers. "One: none of us wants to go to Letterkenny again. Two: even if we do go to the Letterkenny police, I haven't got a flaming licence to show them. Three: That fine is way beyond me. Four: I don't want to rot in an Irish jail."

"What if I find you a good lawyer?"

"Like your dead lawyer? No thanks." Wish-Wash looked at Oodles. "This bloke thinks we've lost our marbles!"

"Why are you so untrusting, Bert?" the Mayor said.

"Hmm, experience? You'd leave me up shit creek without a paddle, and we both know it."

"Well!" The Mayor looked hurt.

"No, you're coming home with us," Wish-Wash said. "Three of us arrived together, they're going to expect all of us to leave together."

Wish-Wash lifted Oodles's bags into the back seat then turned to the Mayor. "I'll give you 10 minutes to get your new toothbrush and whatever else you have or we're leaving without you. It's your choice if you want to stay here but I don't think Cathleen and Shamus are going to be happy when that credit card of yours bounces."

"What!" the Mayor spluttered. "What if they see me leaving?"

"All the more reason to move quickly," Wish-Wash said.

FIFTY-TWO
THE BEST-DRESSED PASSENGER IN GUMBOOTS

THEY DROPPED the car at the Dublin rental-car depot and made it to the airport with plenty of time to catch the flight to London, which would connect to a flight to Melbourne, via Dubai.

Wish-Wash was resplendent again in his lime green suit, but this time he wore flip-flops that showed toenails even more gnarly than before, and he had swapped his tweed cap for his brown and gold Hawthorn beanie again.

No wonder they picked him out for a bag search at security. He looked weird.

The officer went into a tailspin when he discovered the box of toothpaste tubes in Wish-Wash's carry-on bag.

"You can't take these on board, sir."

Wish-Wash eyeballed him back. "Why not?"

"It's forbidden. Would you like to remove your flip-lops and come back round through the X-ray machine?"

"My flip-flops? You can see I'm not hiding more toothpaste in my flaming flip-flops!" Wish-Wash singled out the Mayor standing nearby in his unconventional travelling attire. "Shouldn't you be frisking him? He might be trying to steal potatoes again."

Wish-Wash was the only one frisked though, and he had to lift his arms like he was about to do a starfish jump so the explosives wand could check he wasn't concealing anything nasty in his armpits.

He also had to surrender the box of toothpaste.

They made it to the gate on time — but only just.

———

The Mayor tried his best at Heathrow Airport in London to get his upgrade to business class transferred.

But the woman on the airport desk explained that since the old men were changing their tickets at such short notice, they were actually lucky to even get three economy seats.

"I presume you all want to sit together?" she said. "Give me a few minutes. I'll need to reshuffle some other passengers."

As she studied the screen, the Mayor lowered his voice. "At least that's something. Better sitting next to the buffoons you know than the ones you don't know."

Wish-Wash looked down at him. "You're quite well acquainted with the bloke who peed in a bottle all the way over here. I'll just check if he's flying with us again."

The Mayor grabbed him as he turned to ask. "Don't you dare," he hissed.

Wish-Wash looked at Oodles. "What do you reckon, cobber? Is Jimbo violating the skyway dress-code by wearing that old jumper under his jacket."

Oodles nodded downwards. "I'm more worried about his health. Those gumboots might encourage deep-vein thrombosis though, don't you think?"

"Maybe," Wish-Wash said. "An even greater worry to me is those rubber boots will fill with water if we ditch into the ocean. Whatever you do, don't hang on to him."

"Oh, for goodness sake," the Mayor said. "Are you two going to carry on like this all the way home?"

The woman smiled as she handed them their boarding passes.
The Mayor had the middle seat all the way.

FIFTY-THREE
ELVIS IMPERSONATORS

"I'LL NEED to borrow your phone," Wish-Wash said as they walked down the concourse past other gates at Tullamarine Airport in Melbourne.

"What for?" the Mayor said.

"Why do you think? I need to make an appointment with my chiropodist."

"Really?"

"Of course not, you drongo! I need to call Rod to arrange a lift home when we fly into Launceston."

The Mayor sighed wearily as he took the phone out of his pocket and handed it over. They had been waiting in departure lounges or flying for close to 27 hours. Worse, every time he had tried to lower his seat on the A-380 flight from Dubai, the passenger behind him had banged on the back of the headrest until he had put it upright again. James Northan looked like he just wanted to lie down, which didn't seem likely to happen for a while yet. They had to wile away three more hours in Melbourne before the last flight home.

Wish-Wash stopped at an empty gate to sit down and make his call. He joined them 15 minutes later in the cafe.

Normally he'd be beaming when he laid eyes on a cuppa and a chocolate digestive biscuit waiting for him.

But his frown indicated something was wrong.

"What's the matter, old son?" Oodles said.

"Rod wasn't answering, so I called Katy. After she got over the shock that we're home early, she said she'd come and pick us up instead."

"In her little car? She'll be hard pressed to get us all in."

"Joffa squeezes in there, doesn't he?"

"So where's Rod?" Oodles said.

"Apparently, he's somewhere near Parkes in New South Wales driving around a busload of Elvis impersonators."

"He's what?"

"That's what I said. It helps to explain why he never answered my emails. If he's on the road, he never even got them." He paused for breath. "Katy said she'll fill us in when we get home. She also said they finally caught Messerschmitt while we were away."

On hearing this, the Mayor spat out a spray of tea. "They arrested my nephew?"

Oodles looked hard at him. "You'd better hope his story accords with yours about the burning down of the pub. We wouldn't want to have to visit you in jail again."

The blood drained from James Northan's face.

Oodles turned to Wish-Wash. "What do you think Rod's up to then? I thought you were going to move into his digs at Slutz Plains?"

"So did I." Wish-Wash munched his biscuit.

FIFTY-FOUR
WHAT A SURPRISE!

KATY WAS WAITING for them as they came up the steps inside the terminal at Launceston Airport.

Oodles got the first hug, then Wish-Wash, then the Mayor.

"I didn't think you'd be back so soon," she said.

"Neither did I," the Mayor grumped.

Katy guided them over to the luggage carousel, which hadn't started to roll yet.

Oodles remembered when Launceston Airport didn't even have luggage carousels. The suitcases were unloaded from the plane on to a train of trolleys and these were towed into the terminal by a tractor. Then it was a free-for-all as people got their bags. In those days there were no cute sniffer Beagle dogs jumping from case to case then either. They were much more vigilant now about keeping fruit fly out of Tassie.

"You must all be so tired?" Katy said.

"We sure are." Wish-Wash pointed with his thumb. "These other blokes can probably visualise where they're sleeping tonight, but that's not the case for me." He glared at the Mayor. "I'd even consider the old park bench in the High Street for old time's like but *someone* had it moved."

Katy frowned as she processed this. "Of course! You were counting on moving in with Rod, but he's gone on the road."

"Yes, what's with these Elvis Presley impersonators?" Wish-Wash said.

"Long story. A lot has happened here in the short time you've been away. No use me trying to explain it while you're jet-lagged."

"I won't argue with that," Wish-Wash said. "My head is already spinning."

"Oh, and don't worry. I'll make up the spare bed for you at our place."

Wish-Wash made the Mayor lift the two carry-on bags up to the roof rack, then he egged him on like a weightlifting coach as he hoisted the two heavy cases.

By the end of it, the Mayor had to sit on the tarmac to gasp for air.

"Is he all right?" Katy said.

Wish-Wash leant down and patted the Mayor on the back. "Oh, you thrive on the exercise, don't you, Jimbo?"

Katy tied down the cases and grabbed the last suitcase to stow in the boot. It fell open to reveal nothing but air.

"Don't ask," the Mayor said when he looked up and saw the look on her face.

Oodles sat in the front passenger seat, and Wish-Wash and the Mayor sat in the back.

Katy kept Oodles awake with conversation: questions about the trip mainly.

Wish-Wash and the Mayor obviously had nothing to say to each other. They were snoring before the car reached the Western Junction roundabout.

FIFTY-FIVE
KISSING ENEMIES

Moose, Joffa and Awesome Sauce were waiting outside the museum, and waved as they pulled in.

Katy was lucky to find a space in the congested car park.

Oodles was bewildered. "Who owns all these cars? Customers?"

"I wish." Katy pulled on the hand break and nodded towards the building site next door. "Tradies."

Oodles looked around at all the SUVs and trailers. "Someone should tell Sergeant Stretch to move them on!"

"Oh, he knows. But he's had his hands full around here. I told you: a bit has been happening."

Wish-Wash yawned in the back. "I was dreaming we were going home. Where are we?"

Oodles looked around and saw he was rubbing his eyes. "Look out the window, old son. It's no dream."

Oodles got out first, leaning on his walking stick.

Moose walked up to him and shook his hand. "What brings you home so quickly?"

"Ask him." Oodles pointed to the other side of the car where the man in the lime green suit was getting out.

"Wishy, old man," Moose said. Then he noticed the beanie on the old man's head. "Bit early for footy season, isn't it?" He laughed. "You left us in suspense with your last email. Did the Mayor catch that Tasmanian Tiger you had trapped in that kitchen?"

Wish-Wash pointed through the open car door. "Ask him."

It's then they all saw the Mayor was still asleep. His head was tossed back but he had stopped snoring.

"Is he all right?" Joffa said. "You'd tink he'd have woken up with all dis talking?"

"We're all dog-tired," Oodles said.

Wish-Wash bent down into the car, reached across and shook the Mayor by the shoulder.

Nothing.

He shook him more violently.

Still nothing.

"Out of the way." Joffa darted around the side of the car and opened the door. He caught James Northan's body as it slumped into him.

He grabbed him under the arms, laid him back-down on the ground and put an ear to his chest.

The others converged around them.

"Strewth," Oodles looked at Wish-Wash. "We've killed him, haven't we?"

"Quiet," Joffa commanded. "I tink I can still hear his heart beating."

Katy told Awesome Sauce to go fetch Doctor Jenkins.

Joffa looked up at Moose. "He might get here too late. You'll have to take over."

"Me?" Moose said.

"You did say you did a first-aid course in Risdon Jail."

This then explains how the Mayor awoke to find Moose astride him giving him the kiss of life. Lips on lips.

FIFTY-SIX
KISSING COUSINS
FOUR WEEKS LATER

"Hello Jimbo." Wish-Wash handed the Mayor a bunch of flowers and a bottle of liquor.

James Northan looked down at them with a sneer — as if the blooms looked familiar.

Oodles knew the Mayor's suspicions were right. Wish-Wash had stopped to pick them just outside.

It was the first time they had ever been inside the Mayor's granny flat situated in the lush gardens of his daughter's mansion, which was once his.

Now the Mayor was out of the woods with his health, he faced the prospect of moving to another big house. Sergeant Stretch had laid charges against him and given him a court date. Messerschmitt had claimed the Mayor was indeed the instigator in the torching of the pub.

Oodles had no doubt James would wriggle out of it. He always did. It would be harder with the family lawyer having kicked the bucket, but Maddie would find another slippery barrister.

Wish-Wash handed the Mayor an envelope and laughed. *Hee-haw, hee-haw.*

The Mayor studied both sides. The envelope was blank front and back. He looked up quizzically.

"It contains your DNA results. The first bit of good news is it confirms Conn Northan *is* your relative."

The Mayor spat out his words. "How can they know that? I never even gave them my DNA!"

"You still think someone broke in to our hotel room and stole your toothbrush?"

The Mayor glared at him. "You didn't?" he hissed.

"That's for me to know and for you to find out." Wish-Wash paused. "Anyway, you're not the only one who's not thrilled to have an Irish cousin. When Malachy realised I had skipped town, he was furious."

"How do you know?"

"He made his feelings known in an email. How dare I leave before refurbishing the castle!"

"What did you tell him?" The Mayor said.

"I told him I was relinquishing the castle to him. If he needs to find funding, I told him a Tasmanian Tiger is loose in his vicinity. I told him how Moose said if someone catches a Tasmanian Tiger in Ireland, it's going to be worth a million dollars."

Wish-Wash broke into another smile. "Do you want to hear the second bit of good news? Conn's coming to visit." He paused. "Of course, you mightn't be here." He looked around the room and his grin grew wider. *Hee-haw, hee-haw.* "But I'm sure you'll let him stay here so he can visit you in Risdon on weekends."

———

As it happens, James didn't go to jail.

But what happened next might have been worse.

You'll need to read the next novel in the Windy Mountain series to find out what.

SOME WEEKS LATER

BOOK 5 IN THE WINDY MOUNTAIN SERIES

I had planned to give the three old men a rest from prying eyes for a while — but I didn't count on the pandemic starting.

So rather than pick up their lives at some stage in the future, I put them into lockdown together back in Windy Mountain.

What results is a bit of a black comedy as hitmen and Tasmanian Tigers bunker down with them!

THE PANDEMIC HITS HOME

THE OLD MAN looked up when someone burst through the door of the hospital room.

A sturdy woman wearing a starched white dress marched towards his bed clutching a clipboard.

Sister Daisy Rowbottom glared down at him. "I heard you were in here, James. How was your trip to Ireland?" She nodded towards his daughter, who was sitting in a blue vinyl chair on the other side of the bed. "Morning, Maddie."

James Northan often bumped into Daisy in the aisles of Roses Supermarket. She had earned a reputation as a dragon before she retired from nursing some years ago, but she had mellowed. These days she liked a chat by the frozen peas.

But what was she doing here looking so fearsome again? She had to be well into her seventies. How had she even been able to squeeze into that dress! Her white cap emblazoned with its red cross looked like something she had brought back from a field hospital in the Crimean War.

"Oh, I get it." James stretched back on his pillows, adjusted one of his hearing aids, then put his hand behind him to cradle his head. "You are on your way to a fancy dress party." He smiled. "Let me guess what as? Florence Nightingale? Have you considered taking a lamp along as a prop?"

Daisy's eyes became slits. "This is no time for frivolity, James. I volunteered when they put out a call for trained nurses to help get them through this COVID crisis."

James rolled his eyes. "Oh, not someone else over-reacting!"

Daisy looked down at the clipboard. "Right," she said. "We need to determine who needs to be here and who needs to be discharged."

James wriggled himself further up on his pillows and made a Victory sign with two fingers. "Did you hear that, Maddie? They are letting me go home." He turned his head the other way. "I have had a bit of cardiac trouble, Daisy. But I am tickety-boo now."

"That's not what it says here." Daisy tapped the clipboard with a chubby index finger. "You're lucky a bystander knew how to administer the kiss of life. Otherwise you'd still be dead."

James's smile disappeared. "Reprobates like Moose should not be allowed to learn CPR!"

Daisy spotted the dried blood on the back of James's liver-spotted hand where the cannula had been inserted, and scowled. "Who did that?"

She didn't wait for an answer. "I can see standards have slipped around here." She cleared her throat. "We shall have to do something about that."

Daisy looked down at the clipboard again. "I see this is your third time in Windy Mountain Hospital, James." She read on, looked up and screeched. "What were you thinking checking yourself out? At your age?"

"I am only 82!" he shouted back.

James took a deep breath and lowered his voice. "As I said, I am fine now. Angioplasty worked wonders on me."

"They wouldn't have transferred you back here if they didn't think you needed further bed-rest."

"Bed-rest? You are joking! I had proper bed-rest in Hobart. I had a single room in a private hospital, with good food and doctors who speak English." James's left hand was tethered to an IV machine and it hurt every time he tugged it, but he was able to wave his free fist towards the other bed. "Here I am forced to share."

Daisy looked at the smooth light-blue quilt and the clean, white pillows, then looked back blankly. "No one is even occupying that bed."

"Maybe not. But it is a constant reminder that at any time someone might be wheeled in here in the middle of the night. That is when things happen in this hick hospital. I did not have sleep apnea until I came in here. Now I wake up every 10 minutes with the noise at night."

"Oh, James!"

"Do they not know who I *was*! Who Maddie *is*! The great unwashed should look up to more important individuals who rise to the exalted position of mayor."

"Public hospitals don't play favourites."

"I paid taxes all my life. For what? The food here is disgusting. In Hobart, dinner came with a little bottle of wine. Now I cannot even get a decent cup of tea."

Daisy forced a smile. "I think you're exaggerating, James."

"Am I? Is it any wonder I checked myself out? I would still be recuperating in the tranquility of my own cottage and in the comfort of my own soft bed, if it had not been for those clowns."

"Clowns?" Daisy frowned.

"Bert Whish-Willson and Clarence Noodle had the audacity to visit me."

"I thought you were friends with Wish-Wash and Oodles."

"Just because we sometimes used to sit together on the bench on the High Street does not mean we are kindred spirits." He sounded like a deflating balloon as his breath started running out. "You will find this out soon. The older you get, the more you are forced to mix with whoever is left."

"But didn't you go to Ireland with them?"

"Mistake of my life!" James looked towards the ceiling. "After the way they treated me on that trip, I cannot fathom how they had the bareface cheek to come to my cottage where I was recuperating after my release from this poor excuse for a hospital. Who gives a man flowers, for heaven's sake? To add insult to injury, they picked them from my own garden." He breathed in, then exhaled just as noisily. "And who gives a bottle of Raki to a man who is convalescing unless they are trying to finish him off?"

Daisy spoke slowly. "I'm afraid I don't actually know what Raki is." She glanced at Maddie in search of a clue.

"No use looking at her. Maddie has never been to Crete. Raki is a crude alcoholic drink distilled for a certain clientele. Mainly peasants! You would know it if you smelled it. They probably market it in this country as hospital disinfectant."

The nasty taste in his mouth intensified just thinking about it. "The final straw was when they tried to wind me up by claiming my so-called Irish cousin was on his way to Australia. I showed them the door quick smart, I can tell you."

Daisy glanced down at her clipboard again and flipped over the page. "That's when you had your second collapse?"

James tried to rearrange a pillow by reaching behind with his untethered hand. Maddie reacted to his grunt of frustration by getting to her feet, and sliding the pillow behind his back. But he didn't thank her, preferring to keep up his tirade towards Daisy. "Can you blame me? I was supposed to be keeping my blood pressure down."

Daisy kept looking at Dr Rashidmanhi's notes. "You know, not everyone actually makes it to the Windy Mountain Hospital in the back of that ambulance. Some have to finish their trip in the back of a roadside assistance truck."

James shook his fist. "That ambulance was state of the art when we bought it. I should know. I was chairman of the hospital board in those days."

"You'd know it was an ice-cream van in its former life then?" Daisy said. "Why do you think they were happy to get rid of it? It's not good for business when your ice-cream van keeps breaking down and the soft-serve all melts."

"I'm here, am I not?"

Daisy shuffled to the end of the bed and hung the clipboard on the rail. "You're right. You are here. We'll just have to make the best of it." She sighed. "I can see you've had a bad run, too. We all know what stress Messerschmitt caused you, now these health issues beset you."

In the next breath, she said: "You won't mind if we put someone else in this room? We might even have to squeeze a third bed in if things get really bad."

"Over my dead body!" James's eyes strained against their sockets. "I'm not sharing my room with riff-raff."

"You won't have a choice if it gets as bad as we're expecting."

"In that case, I *demand* to go home."

"I think not," Daisy said, lifting her chins. "You're what we call an essential patient."

"People were right about you," James hissed. "You are nothing but a bossy old spinster who likes to control your patient's lives."

Daisy's eyes darkened. For a long time, she said nothing. Then she said slowly: "You *will* tell me if you can't move your bowels, Mr Northan. Perhaps the nurse who butchered the insertion of your cannula also needs to practise doing enemas."

———

He watched her stride out of the room, then locked eyes with Maddie. "That is it. I'm checking myself out again."

"Is that a good idea, Daddy? You know what happened last time."

"I would have been fine if those fools had not come visiting."

"I'm sure they meant the best."

"This time I will put a padlock on the gate."

Maddie gave an exasperated sigh. "The doctors have only just got your blood pressure back under control. You heard Daisy. They won't let you check out so easily this time."

"I am not — I emphasise *not* — sharing my room with sick people. Besides, you heard her. She has become a tyrant again."

"You just hate being outbullied, Daddy!"

"What's that supposed to mean? At least I have the courtesy to listen to people before telling them what to do."

Maddie rolled her eyes.

James rotated his hand to show the dried blood. "Daisy really could not care less an incompetent nurse has used me as a darts board. She just wants to resume her reign of terror."

"Oh Daddy."

"Do not *Daddy* me. She could easily organise a line-up of nurses so I could identify the culprit. But no, she would rather humiliate the lot of them to show them who is boss."

James sighed heavily. "That is how she operates. You heard her threaten me with an enema."

Maddie gave a little laugh. "I think you'll find she was only joking."

"People thought it was a medical miracle the day she retired, and patients' stress levels all dropped."

———

Maddie steepled her fingers and squeezed her eyes shut. "I didn't want to have to tell you this, Daddy . . ."

"Tell me what?"

"You *can't* go home."

James opened his eyes wide, so wide it hurt. "Why not?"

Maddie opened her eyes. "I didn't think you'd mind. He said he had no where else to stay."

James tugged at a strand of his straggly, thin hair. "Who?"

"Your cousin."

"My cousin? Which cousin?"

"Your cousin from Ireland."

"Conn? I thought Bert and Clarence were just trying to wind me up." He stared into space. "Where does a bog Irishman like that even get the money to travel?"

"He arrived two days ago," Maddie said. "The State Government insists that all new arrivals to the state self-isolate for 14 days."

James buried his head in his free hand, and hissed: "You let him infect my cottage!"

"If your nephew hadn't burnt down the hotel . . ."

James looked up. "At least you know for sure Messerschmitt *is* your cousin. You do not know the Irishman from Adam. What were you thinking inviting him to stay?"

"I could hardly tell him to go sleep under the bridge. How would that look? I have an election coming up. Remember?"

"What about a hotel in another town? Is it not about time Sltutz Plains took a share of Irish people?"

"He's flesh and blood."

"The jury is out on that. All we know for sure is his DNA matches the DNA found on my toothbrush. Bert Whish-Willson is not too fussy about which toothbrush he uses."

"But the Irishman's last name is Northan. You don't think that's a hint?"

"I don't think it is conclusive, no."

"I thought you'd be fine with it, especially seeing as you'd be in here for at least another two weeks."

"Is he showing symptoms of actually being sick?"

Maddie shrugged. "He's not answering my phone calls, or the door."

James banged his fist down on the bed. "Just what I need? A corpse in my cottage!"

"He can't be dead, Daddy. We can see the lights going on and off from our house."

"So you are letting him run up my electricity bills?" He rolled his eyes. "Great!"

Maddie folded her arms. "You can't go there now. If you insist on checking out of here, I'll just have to make other arrangements."

AUTHOR'S NOTE

THE WINDY MOUNTAIN Tasmanian Tiger series has made it into more than 80 countries, so I must be doing something right.

This is the first time though I've taken my characters into another country.

I've visited Ireland a couple of times. So, yes, I did borrow from my own experiences. I dream of Donegal on hot days in Canberra.

FINALLY

This novel has been professionally edited. If you've got this far my guess is you've successfully navigated the Australian spelling, slang and deliberate oddities. But typos always manage to slip through the net, so by all means let me know if something's out of order.

– John Martin
https://johnmartin-author.blog

MY BOOKS

Windy Mountain series

Lie of the Tiger (#1)

He's not who he says he is. Who will rescue him?

———

Blokes on a Plane (#2)

Why is the mayor speaking old English? And where has he disappeared to?

―――

Whitey and the Six Dwarfs (#3)

Troupe of Elvis impersonators come to the rescue.

———

Blokes in Donegal (#4)

Three old blokes go to Ireland hoping to discover family history. The mayor had to take his great, great, great grandfather's head, didn't he!

———

Blokes in the House (#5)

How the old blokes coped with COVID quarantine (clue: the major didn't).

———

Who Knew Tasmanian Tigers Eat Apples. (#6)

Back to before the beginning. Wish-Wash leads a public revolt.

_____

Who Knew Tiger Sharks also Eat Apples? (#7)

A character from the old days returns in an unlikely guise. It's all about comic revenge.

———

The Life and Deaths of Billy Gumboots (#8)

'His foot, my boot.'

———

Blokes Send in the Clones (#9)

Two old blokes have a crack at cloning a Tasmanian tiger.

To come:

10 — Blokes do the Block

Someone marries, someone dies. Might even be the same old bloke.

———

The Wrong Magician (#1)

This time he has to make himself disappear.

———

Daddy's Great Escape (#2)

If Mad Bill hates people so much, why does he make it so hard for them to leave his island?

Escape from Mad Bill's Island (#3)

He came seeking to find out what the British were up to on the island in World War 2. He won't like the answer.

———

Major B.S. comes to the end of his Rope

It all started when he rescued the wrong group of people from a prisoner-of-war camp. It just becomes worse.

———